DRAGON DETECTIVE

THAT'S A WRAP!

GARETH P. JONES

Brant Buchanan kicked off his expensive shoes, loosened his silk tie and reclined on the plush leather back seat of his car. Outside, the Californian sun was heating up the boulevard but the billionaire's car was as cool as an English spring morning. Brant's driver and confidante, Weaver, sat at the wheel.

"LA is far too hot," said Brant. "Please tell me you've discovered something."

"I have located a pair of – *ahem* – experts in the area who should be able to help," Weaver replied, "but I must warn you, they are a little eccentric."

"Given the subject matter, I would expect nothing less," said Buchanan. He pushed one of the many glowing buttons in the car door and a panel opened.

1

He reached in and pulled out a book. It was a red hardback with a white zigzag across the cover. If there had ever been a dustjacket it had long since been lost. There was no title or author's name on the cover, but on the first page were the words:

Dragonlore
A Scientific Study of Dragons
By Ivor Klingerflim

"This is such a fascinating book, Weaver," said Buchanan. "For example, did you know that dragon mothers plant their eggs in the liquid fire of Earth's Inner Core, then wait on the banks for the young dragon to swim to the surface?"

"No, sir, I didn't," replied Weaver, whose lack of enthusiasm for his boss's latest project hadn't stopped him carrying out his orders efficiently and unquestioningly. Indeed, it was he who had obtained this copy of the book.

"Listen to this bit," said Buchanan. "*The term 'up-airer' relates to a great Himalayan conference, held a thousand years ago when those dragons in favour of destroying mankind rose into the air (and became known as up-airers). Luckily for humans, the majority stayed on the ground and so dragonkind went into hiding."*

"Fascinating, sir," said Weaver.

Mr Buchanan continued to read aloud. *"In spite of this, many dragons believe that war between humans and dragons is inevitable and that they will be led into battle by a dragon carrying the Turning Stone, a large spherical rock which is said to grant power over all dragonkind."*

"It all sounds rather … erm, unbelievable," said Weaver. "Shall I take you back to Sands Hall?"

"Yes, please," replied Buchanan.

"It may take some time. The traffic in LA is particularly bad this evening."

"That's because no one walks in this city." Buchanan looked out at the five lanes of traffic, all moving at a snail's pace under the cloudless sky. A thick layer of hazy pollution hung over the city.

He pressed a button and a drink appeared from the side door. He pushed another and a screen flickered to life, showing grainy CCTV footage. Buchanan picked up the drink and sat back to watch. It showed an office from three different angles. A dragon dropped into the room, looked around and then reached up and lowered a young girl in too.

"I never tire of watching this," he said.

"Yes, but shouldn't we be using the girl to get to the dragon?" enquired Weaver. "There's clearly a connection between them."

"In business I always find it best to arm myself with as much information as possible before making an acquisition," replied Buchanan, "but yes, perhaps it is time to make good use of young Holly Bigsby."

PROD

2

DIR
CAM

On the other side of the Atlantic, a red-backed, green-bellied, urban-based Mountain Dragon called Dirk Dilly was crouching on a roof. He was perfectly camouflaged with the red tiles of a building across the road from a warehouse in east London.

A high wire fence surrounded the warehouse with a sign that read, **DANGER: DEMOLITION IN PROGRESS**. A number of workers in yellow bibs and hard hats had already reduced most of a neighbouring warehouse to rubble. One of the men was operating a large red machine that looked like an enormous crab's claw attached to the base of a tank. He pulled a lever and the claw crashed into the last remaining wall of the destroyed building. The claw snapped shut, crushing bricks and sending clouds of dust into the air.

It had all started that morning while Dirk had been keeping an eye on a skyscraper in central London. Unknown to its human occupants, it was being used as a base by Vainclaw Grandin's Kinghorns, a group of dragons intent on waging war upon humanity, which is why Dirk had been watching the building.

After weeks of surveillance, he had finally spotted something. A Sea Dragon by the name of Flotsam had appeared on top of the building. When no one was looking, he had spread his wings and glided down, over Dirk's head, landing on a nearby church. Dirk had followed Flotsam across the city to a warehouse in east London. He knew this place. It was another of the Kinghorns' hideouts. Flotsam had entered the building unseen but Dirk was anxious to avoid being spotted by the demolition crew.

The foreman blew a whistle.

"Tea's up!" he shouted, and all the workers, including the man operating the claw, headed towards a cabin on the far side of the site.

Dirk took his opportunity and leaped from the

rooftop, touching a foot on the top of the claw machine, spring-boarding up into the air and landing on the flat roof of the warehouse.

He peered in through the dirty skylight.

Below were the four crates he had seen on his first visit to this warehouse all those months ago, with the words **DO NOT OPEN** printed in red on the top. In the middle of the crates was a Mountain Dragon — red-backed and green-bellied just like Dirk himself. His name was Jegsy Grandin and he was the nephew of Vainclaw. He had a yellow hard hat balanced on his head and was talking to Flotsam.

Dirk prized the skylight open and slipped inside. Sticking to the rafters, he closed it behind him as quietly as possible and blended.

"Jegsy, you have to listen to sense. We've got to get out of here," said Flotsam. "They're going to flatten this place with you in it."

"My uncle said to stay here until I hear from him," protested Jegsy.

"Listen, Jegsy, Vainclaw's gone underground. No one's heard from him for weeks. Forget the Kinghorns.

There's a new movement and we're calling ourselves One-Worlders."

"What's one of them then?"

"I'll tell you on the way."

Outside, the crushing machine started up again and the shouts of the workmen could be heard. There was an enormous crash, which shook the building so violently that the colour returned to Dirk's skin for a moment. Luckily, neither Jegsy nor Flotsam noticed.

Suddenly, the red metal of the large claw came through the side of the building. It withdrew, causing bits of brick to fall down. One of them landed on Jegsy's head, bouncing off his hard hat and whacking Flotsam in the face.

"Ye-ouch!" cried Jegsy.

"Come on, Jegs." Flotsam jumped into a crate.

Jegsy jumped into another. "I don't like this one bit."

"You haven't exactly got a choice. Come on."

They both spoke a few words in Dragonspeak, asking the rock to take them down. The rock, being rock, complied and they vanished down into the earth.

A second crash rocked the building, causing Dirk to lose his grip and fall to the ground. Bits of wood and concrete landed on top of him. The machine had made a large hole in the corner of the building. Dirk jumped up and shook the dust off his back. He ran around the crates, knocking them away. Beneath each one was solid rock. They would all lead to tunnels far below London, but Dirk couldn't afford to bump into the Dragnet officers who would be patrolling them. The last time Dirk had come into contact with them, he had wound up in prison. He had managed to escape with the help of a Sea Dragon called Alba Longs and a yellow-bellied, coal-black Cave Dweller called Fairfax Nordstrum, but he didn't fancy repeating the experience.

There was a terrible scraping as the machine continued to chew away at the building. Dirk moved to a boarded-up window, where he could see the yellow of the workmen's bibs through the slats. He was surrounded.

Another crash from outside dislodged a metal pipe and caused a hissing sound. Dirk recognized the smell. Gas. Someone had forgotten to disconnect it before knocking the building down. This was a dangerous mistake but something Dirk could use to his advantage. He lifted an overturned crate with his tail, grabbed it with his free paw and placed it over the pipe, meaning the escaping gas filled the crate.

There was a **KRA-SMASH** as the crunching machine came through a window. Dirk could hear the workmen shouting. He had to act quickly before they got too close. He didn't want anyone getting hurt. The gas was seeping through the gaps of the crate. The crunching machine took hold of a section of the building and twisted, mangling a mass of metal rods that ran through the wall. The whole structure shook, causing the skylight to crack and shards of glass to shower on to Dirk. He flew up to the hole in the roof.

"Here goes nothing," he said.

He looked down at the crate, took aim, opened his mouth and exhaled. Dirk's fire caught the escaping vapours of gas, drawing flames down into the crate.

There was a moment's silence that felt like an intake of breath.

"Take cover!" yelled Dirk.

And then…

A flash of light.

The sound of the explosion filled the air and the surrounding workmen dived to the ground to protect themselves from the blast. Lying down, covering their faces, none of them noticed the four-metre-long, red-backed, green-bellied, urban-based Mountain Dragon flying over their heads.

PROD

3

DIR
CAM

Holly had been imprisoned in her house since she had returned home late at night a few weeks ago, her jeans torn and covered in blood but with no visible sign of injury. Her parents had demanded to know where she had been and what had happened.

"And we want the truth," her dad had said sternly.

Telling the truth would have involved her admitting that her leg had been broken while clinging on to a dragon's back as he flew up a lift shaft. When they asked why the broken bone was no longer broken she would have had to admit that it was fixed by a Sky Dragon called Nebula Colorado.

Sometimes the truth wasn't an option.

As a punishment, she had been grounded for the

whole summer holiday. No television, no internet and no leaving the house until school began in September. Holly felt like a caged animal, which was why she had taken to sneaking downstairs to watch TV late at night while her parents were asleep.

She slipped into the front room, switched on the TV and turned the volume down. She couldn't afford to wake them. They had made it perfectly clear what would happen if she was discovered out of her room.

"One step out of line and I'm sending you back to William Scrivener's," Dad had said. Holly had hated her time at the rich-kid boarding school, sharing a room with Petal Moses, away from London, away from Willow, her cat, and away from Dirk.

She flicked through the channels. It was the usual late-night programming: a reality TV show, an American detective film and an unfunny sitcom. Holly stopped on a channel showing a female presenter with big hair and a smile set to full beam, sitting behind a desk with *Hollywood Gossip* written behind her.

"What are your children doing this summer?" chirruped the presenter happily. "Whatever it is, I bet it won't be as exciting as it is for one very special twelve-year-old, currently here in Hollywood making a movie all about herself. It could only be Petal Moses, pop's most precocious offspring."

A picture of Holly's former roommate appeared behind the presenter. She looked tanned, had a fancy new haircut and was sporting a nose ring.

"The movie in question? It's the adaptation of Petal's autobiography, *When Petals Blossom*. The film – with its working title, *Petal: The Movie* – will star young Miss Moses in the title role and will be directed by legendary Hollywood film director, Chase Lampton."

A man with thick, curly black hair, wearing sunglasses and a leather jacket, appeared on the screen. "To me it's more than a movie about the child of a pop-star-slash-actress," said the man. "It's kind of an analysis of celebrity culture."

It cut back to the presenter. "Lampton will also be directing his own son, Dante Lampton." The screen behind her showed the director standing next to a boy who looked like a scaled-down version of him. "And talking of keeping things in the family, can you guess who's providing the soundtrack as well as picking up an executive producer credit? Of course, it's Petal's famous mother..."

Holly switched channels. She hated Petal. The spoilt popstar's daughter got everything she ever wanted and probably always would. Holly wasn't jealous that Petal was making a film or that she was in Hollywood, but she did envy her freedom.

Hearing the door creak, she quickly switched off the TV and froze, using her dragon skills to blend with the sofa. But the footsteps that entered the room were too light to be Dad or Mrs Bigsby. Holly's head reappeared as she turned to see a black cat with a white face and a black smudge on her nose padding into the room. She reached down and scooped her up.

"Hello, Willow," Holly said, stroking her cat and noticing that her fur was cold. "You've been outside, have you?" she said into her ear. "Lucky thing."

Willow meowed in reply and Holly noticed something attached to her collar. It was a biro case but instead of a pen inside there was a rolled-up piece of paper.

"What have you got here?" Holly removed the biro

and pulled out the piece of paper. She unfurled it and read the scrawled note:

COME TO THE CAT FLAP

Holly crept to the kitchen. She crouched down and looked through the cat flap to find her best friend, Archie Snellgrove, blinking back at her, his unkempt dirty blond hair falling over his face.

"What are you doing here?" she asked.

"Can I come in? It's really cold," said Archie, shivering.

PROD

4

DIR
CAM

Back in the safety of his office, Dirk sat with his feet on the desk, sipping a cocktail of orange and blackcurrant squash. On the TV was one of his all-time favourite American detective films *The Big Zero*. It was a classic and the reason Dirk had become a detective in the first place. He blew a smoke ring and relaxed.

"Mr Dilly, are you awake?" whispered a shaky voice from outside his door.

"Wide awake, Mrs Klingerflim," said Dirk.

The door opened and his elderly landlady's owl-like face appeared.

"Sorry to bother you so late, Mr Dilly," she said.

"I've always got time for you, Mrs K," he replied.

"Oh, you are sweet," said Mrs Klingerflim, removing her thick glasses and wiping the lenses. Dirk noticed how old and fragile she looked without them. She put them back on and said, "That's better, now I can see you."

For years, Dirk had assumed that Mrs Klingerflim was so blind that she thought he was human. It had come as a complete surprise to learn that she not only knew he was a dragon, but his exact subspecies, due to having spent years dragon-spotting with her late husband, Ivor. She even helped write his definitive guide to dragons, *Dragonlore*.

"I was worried you might be sleeping," said the old lady. "My dear Ivor was a very light sleeper. He used to say that a whispering ant could wake him up." She shook her head fondly. "I'm the complete opposite. An elephant with a foghorn couldn't rouse me. Although, now I think about it, I'm not sure an elephant could operate a foghorn ... unless it was one of those trained ones from the circus. Not that you can have animals working in circuses these days."

"Sorry, Mrs K, did you want me for something?" replied Dirk, assuming that she hadn't popped in to talk about elephants.

"Oh yes, I'm sorry. Things fly in and out of my head like paper aeroplanes sometimes," she said. "Would you mind checking the cellar? There's a funny noise. I'm worried we might have rats in there or something. I'd go down myself but the steps are very steep and the doctor says I shouldn't take any unnecessary risks at my age, what with my knees and ankles."

On the TV, two men were watching a burning building.

"Hold on, my favourite line is coming up," said Dirk.

"I used to love the movies," said Mrs Klingerflim. "What's this one about then?"

"They're brothers who run a detective agency. That was their office. You find out later that the one on the right paid someone to burn it down, but we don't know that yet," said Dirk.

There was a close-up of the man, his face reflecting the flickering yellow light from the fire. As he spoke, Dirk said the line along with him.

"You realize, Joe, that everything we worked for over these past ten years has just gone up in smoke? Let's go get a bagel."

"Brilliant," said Dirk, following Mrs Klingerflim out of the room and down the stairs. As usual, Dirk was careful to make sure his scaly skin didn't knock off the photos that lined the wall. He glanced at them as he slowly followed Mrs Klingerflim down and noticed a picture of his landlady when she was much younger, standing in front of a large rock, smiling at the camera. She had her arms linked with a man, who had a wide grin, deep dimples and kind eyes.

"Is this Ivor?" he asked. He realized that, after all his landlady had told him about her husband, he didn't even know what he looked like.

Mrs Klingerflim turned round and climbed back up one stair. She pulled the picture off the wall and squinted at it. There was a white line across it where the camera lens had been scratched. She turned it round and read the back at arm's length. "Oh, that's right," she said, "that was one of our little trips. They were happy days. I do miss him, Mr Dilly."

Dirk felt uncomfortable. He wasn't used to human feelings. Things were simpler for dragons. What family connections existed were easily severed. Dragons didn't fall in love or get married.

"So, the cellar…" he said awkwardly.

"Yes, the cellar," said Mrs Klingerflim, pulling herself out of her thoughts.

They continued in silence to the bottom of the stairs and round the corner to the cellar door. Dirk pushed it open and looked down.

"I can't hear anything," he said.

"It comes and goes," replied Mrs Klingerflim.

"I'll go and have a look. Where's the light switch?" he asked.

"It's on the wall, but it won't do you any good. The bulb's blown. I've been meaning to change it but the doctor said I shouldn't be standing on chairs and things with my hips."

"No problem, I'll make my own light," said Dirk, opening his mouth to breathe fire.

"I'd rather you didn't," said the old lady. "There are a few sentimental things down there and I fear they may be rather flammable. I've found you a torch." She handed him a black plastic torch. Dirk switched it on and headed down the stairs.

In the cellar, he swung the torch around. There were boxes full of notebooks and scraps of paper.

He picked up a notepad from under a curved paperweight and flicked through it. It was full of sketches of dragons. "What is all this stuff?" he shouted up the stairs.

"Ivor's notes for the book. I know it's silly but I couldn't bear to throw it all away."

Dirk stopped at a page with a line drawing of a dragon with hundreds of thin spikes covering its back. At the bottom of the page Ivor had written, *Californian Desert Dragon – 1973.*

"Can you hear anything now?" called Mrs Klingerflim.

"Nothing yet," said Dirk. "What sort of noise was it?"

"It sounded like a kind of scratching."

Dirk placed the notepad back on the pile and looked around.

"There it goes," said Mrs Klingerflim.

Dirk listened. Sure enough, there was a quiet scratching coming from behind a faded wooden cabinet in a dark corner of the cellar. The old lady's eyesight may have been failing but her hearing was fine.

Dirk moved quietly towards it and gently eased open the cabinet doors. He was bracing himself for rats. Dirk wasn't a big fan of rats, but the eyes staring out at him were too big to belong to a rat and the skin was scaly rather than furry.

"Hi, Dirk," whispered Karnataka Cuddlums, his unreliable friend.

"Have you found anything, Mr Dilly?" called Mrs Klingerflim.

Dirk looked down at the Shade-Hugger's brown head inside the base of the cabinet.

"It's just as we thought," he shouted. "A rat."

5

Holly felt bad for Archie, crouched outside the house.
He looked freezing and it was beginning to rain, but
what could she do?

"The door's locked and the alarm is on," she said.
"You know how serious they are about keeping me
in."

"How about I climb in through a window?" he
suggested.

"No. The whole place is shut up like a prison. You
have to go home," insisted Holly.

"I can't. Things aren't so good there right now."
Before Holly could ask why, Archie added, with a
forced grin, "Are you telling me that they've locked
up this place so tightly that even the great Holly

Bigsby can't get round it?"

"Well, obviously I've considered it..." Holly smiled back. "Stay there."

She let go of the cat flap and made her way up the stairs.

Her parents had taken great precautions to prevent her leaving, including installing a security system for all the doors and windows, but Holly had a plan.

Mrs Bigsby changed the alarm code every day. She stored the latest code on her phone, which was usually slipped inside the top drawer of her bedside table, along with the keys. She had always slept with a phone nearby. Back when she worked as a politician, she had to take calls at any time of day or night. Since she had started working for the billionaire Brant Buchanan, she hardly got any calls. In spite of this, Holly had noticed her stepmum constantly checking her phone. Sometimes she got Mr Bigsby to call it to test it was still working. Judging by the antique furniture she had ordered and the talk of a new kitchen, she was getting paid well enough but she didn't work anywhere near as hard as before.

Holly darted up the stairs, careful to avoid the noisy floorboards, and across the landing to the bedroom door. She pushed it open and poked her head round the corner, ready to freeze and blend if either of them stirred.

Her dad was snoring lightly. Mrs Bigsby was sleeping with her face disconcertingly near to where the keys rested on the bedside table. Holly approached. She noticed that her stepmother's eyes were only half shut. For a moment Holly thought that she was awake, but she quickly realized that her eyes weren't focusing on her and from the rhythmic breathing, it was clear that she was asleep.

Since accidentally acquiring a dragon claw, Holly had taken to wearing it around her neck, and she was aware of it as she reached over and picked up the keys. She clasped a hand over them to stop them jangling, then eased the drawer open and extracted the phone.

Mrs Bigsby let out a small moan. "Yes, granite surfaces and wood floors," she muttered in her sleep. Holly could feel her heart pounding against the dragon claw as she made her way across the room, out of the door and down the stairs, where she pulled out the phone and unlocked it. The screen lit up.

78 missed calls

She dismissed the message and searched through the contacts until she found Mr A Code.

"Mr A Code," she said to herself, smiling. "Alarm code. Subtle!"

Sure enough, Mr Code's telephone number was only four digits long. She opened the cupboard under the stairs where the alarm was kept and typed the numbers into the keypad. The alarm let out a long beep to indicate that it had been switched off.

Holly ran to the back door, unlocked and opened it.

"Under five minutes, not bad," said Archie, looking at his watch.

"Shh," hushed Holly. "Come in." She shut the door behind Archie and locked it before following him into the living room.

"Do you know how much trouble I'm in if we're found out?" she said.

Archie reached into his pocket and offered Holly a jellybean.

"No, thanks," she said.

"Sorry. I had nowhere else to go." He threw the sweet into his mouth.

"Stay here," she said, unlocking a window to give Archie an easy way out. "I'm going to put everything back then I'll come down again."

"You want help?" offered Archie.

"It's easier alone. I'll be back in a second," replied Holly, slipping out into the hallway, up the stairs and into the bedroom. She replaced the keys on the bedside table first, then dropped the phone into the drawer. She turned to leave but a buzzing noise stopped her. Someone was calling the phone. Her stepmum murmured in her sleep. Scared that it would wake her up, Holly reached back inside the drawer and lifted it out to turn it off. The screen displayed the caller's identity.

BRANT BUCHANAN CALLING

ANSWER   DECLINE

She declined the call and immediately felt a hand on her shoulder. She spun round to see her dad standing behind her, looking angry and confused.

"Holly, what on earth are you doing?" he whispered.

In Mrs Klingerflim's cellar, Dirk raised a claw to his lips to indicate to Karnataka to stay quiet.

"Do you want a cup of tea, Mr Dilly?" called Mrs Klingerflim from upstairs.

"Yes, please," he responded. "Two sugars, please, Mrs K."

Dirk waited until he heard the old lady shuffle away to the kitchen and switch on the radio before addressing the Shade-Hugger. "This is interesting behaviour for the captain of the Dragnet," he said in a hushed voice. "Or have the councillors finally seen sense and sacked you?"

"Sacked me?" whined Karnataka. "Those old dragons love me. They're talking about giving me a special commendation."

Dirk couldn't help but smile. "All this time you've spent on the wrong side of the law and it turns out you're better suited to working for the good guys," he said.

"I know," replied Karnataka, with a shrug. "Who'd have thought it?"

"So you're an honest dragon these days, are you?" asked Dirk.

"I'm doing the job well," insisted Karnataka.

Dirk gave his old friend a look of disbelief.

"Well, of course, being captain there are still plenty of opportunities to make an extra bit of gold to … you know … supplement my wage."

Dirk smiled. "I'm relieved. For a minute there I thought you'd gone all respectable on me," he said.

"Look, I'd appreciate it if you didn't go shooting your mouth off about certain things."

"You mean like the time you stole the council's Welsh gold reserves?"

"Exactly, I'm a changed dragon."

"I find that difficult to believe, since you're currently in my landlady's cellar with your head jammed inside a cabinet. What are you doing here?"

"I came to find you. The rock brought me most of the way but these human settlements have concrete foundations. You ever tried talking to concrete? It's a very one-sided conversation, I can tell you. So I had to claw my way through. Give me a hand, will you?"

"My heart bleeds. You shouldn't be here," said Dirk.

Crackly old jazz music drifted downstairs and Dirk could hear Mrs Klingerflim shuffling around the kitchen, singing along.

"Neither of us should be here," said Karnataka. "I don't need to remind you that lodging with a human is a blatant breach of the forbidden divide. If you ever found yourself in front of the Dragon Council you'd be banished to the earth's Inner Core quicker than you could say liquorice laces. Now, please help me up, Dirk, I need to speak to you properly."

"Oh, all right then." Dirk gave in and moved the cabinet, revealing the hole that Karnataka had made in the bottom of Mrs Klingerflim's basement. He reached down and grabbed a claw that the Shade-Hugger had forced into the room, then, with an almighty tug, yanked him into the cellar. Bits of concrete flew all over the place and Dirk fell backwards as the full weight of the Shade-Hugger landed on top of him.

"Get off me!" snarled Dirk.

Karnataka jumped off but landed on an old dressing table, crushing it under his weight, sending splintered wood everywhere.

"Is everything all right down there, Mr Dilly?" called Mrs Klingerflim from the top of the stairs.

"Fine, Mrs K. I just slipped."

"Please be careful, Mr Dilly," she said nervously. "I know it all looks like rubbish but there are lots of things that are very valuable to me down there. My mother gave me that dressing table as a wedding gift. I'll leave your cup of tea at the top of the stairs here."

"She got any liquorice?" asked Karnataka, taking in his surroundings. He lifted a piece of paper. "Hey, this looks like a Limpworm," he said, holding up a line-drawing of a snake-like creature. "What is all this stuff?"

"This stuff is none of your business," said Dirk, snatching it from him. "Why are you here, Karny?"

"What do you know about Minertia?" asked Karnataka.

"The same everyone knows," replied Dirk.

Minertia Tidfell was the oldest, wisest and most powerful dragon of all. She was the one who called the great conference, then counted the vote and announced that dragons would go into hiding. She defined the three aspects of the forbidden divide as being seen by a human, attacking a human or allowing a human to find any evidence of the existence of dragons. Then, years later, she was convicted of breaching it and banished to eternity in the Inner Core.

"Did you ever meet her?"

"No. I saw her at the great conference but I was pretty young then. What's all this about?" said Dirk.

"A dragon that old and powerful must have accumulated a fair amount of treasure, don't you think?" Karnataka's yellow eyes seemed to turn golden, as though reflecting all that imagined wealth.

"Ah, I knew it. It's about gold. Is this one of those opportunities to … how did you put it? Supplement your wage?"

"No," protested Karnataka. "The Kinghorns are gathering support."

"I heard there was a new lot calling themselves One-Worlders."

"Oh, there are a hundred different splinter groups but all of them agitators, and all of them want war."

"What's this got to do with Minertia's treasure?" asked Dirk.

"Vainclaw's cronies are looking for it. I guess he's looking for gold to buy support. So we need to find it first. I've been looking through the records from her trial. Did you know the council offered to reduce her sentence if she told them where it was?"

"If no one's found it in all the years that she's been banished I'm guessing it's pretty well hidden."

"That's why I need you," said Karnataka. "Please, Dirk. You're the best there is."

"No way. Now, get out of here."

Karnataka let out a frustrated growl. "You're making a big mistake, Dirk," he said, but he climbed back into the hole and left Dirk alone in the empty cellar.

Holly and Archie sat silently watching the kettle boil, while Mr Bigsby found a mug and a teabag. Once he had made a cup of tea and poured Archie a glass of milk, he sat down and sighed. Mrs Bigsby's phone lay on the table in front of them.

"I'm sorry, Mr Bigsby, sir," said Archie.

"You're a good lad," he replied. "Holly doesn't have many friends so I'd be all for allowing you to come round but not like this. It's the middle of the night. Your parents must be beside themselves with worry. Maybe I should call them."

"No, please," said Archie. "Things … they aren't so good at home right now."

"What do you mean?" asked Mr Bigsby.

Archie stared back sullenly, refusing to answer the question. Holly desperately wanted to change the subject and shift the focus from her friend. Whatever his problems at home, she understood that he didn't want to talk about it, so she was relieved when the phone buzzed again.

Mr Bigsby peered at the screen. Once again, it read:

BRANT BUCHANAN CALLING

ANSWER   DECLINE

"Maybe I should wake her up," said Mr Bigsby. "It must be urgent to keep trying."

"Yes, you will need to wake up your wife presently," said the unmistakable voice of Brant Buchanan from the phone.

"It answered itself," said Archie.

"An excellent observation, Mr Snellgrove."

"How do you know my name?"

The billionaire's face appeared on the phone.

"Knowledge is as buyable as anything and I have acquired a great amount of it over the years, but you

37

are not my concern at the moment. Mr Bigsby, I need you and your family to drop everything and join me here."

"Where's here?" asked Holly's dad.

"Los Angeles. I have a private jet waiting."

"America!" exclaimed Holly.

"Cool," said Archie.

"I see," said Mr Bigsby. "But we'll have to return the boy first. And we'll have to pack … and find passports and—"

"Malcolm," said Mr Buchanan. "You are aware of how much I pay your wife, I assume. I am not a man who likes to be kept waiting. A car will collect you in twenty minutes and you will be taken to the jet."

"What about Archie?" said Holly.

"I can't go home. Not right now," he replied. "Things aren't so—"

"Oh, just bring your friend," interrupted Mr Buchanan. "Time is of the essence. My people will contact your guardians and make the necessary arrangements. There is no need for passports."

"You mean I can come to America?" said Archie.

"Mr Snellgrove," said the billionaire, "you are an

irrelevance. But yes, you can come."

"Yay!" cried Archie.

Holly didn't know what to think. She was going to America. She was leaving the house and she was going with her best friend, but why? Surely if Brant needed her stepmum for some reason he would just fly her out there? He didn't seem the sort of person to be concerned about splitting up a family.

When she had first encountered him, she had suspected him of being involved with the dragon plot to attack humans but she had been wrong. Still, she didn't like him. He was responsible for companies that experimented on animals and, from what she had seen when she had broken into his top-secret laboratory, he was working on some pretty dubious projects.

Holly wished she could talk to Dirk but that would have to wait. Right now, she needed to find her toothbrush.

Brant Buchanan disconnected the call and stepped out of the car, which was parked outside a laundrette. As he approached he realized that, although he had passed many such establishments in his life, he had never set foot inside one before.

Inside, two ladies were folding sheets. They stopped as he entered and turned to look at him. In his designer clothes and expensive shoes, Brant Buchanan clearly wasn't their usual customer.

"Can I help you?" one of them said.

"I'm looking for Frank Precious," he replied.

The women looked at each other, then burst into hysterics. Brant Buchanan felt a rare sensation of discomfort.

"That's two people, sweetie, and they're through that door," said the other woman.

"Thank you." Buchanan found a door with a piece of paper pinned on it. It read:

Frank Precious
Inexplicable Investigations
Please knock before entering

Buchanan turned the handle.

"Aren't you going to knock?" asked the first lady.

"I'm expected." Buchanan opened the door and

stepped into a dark room.

"Nooo!" cried a voice inside. "Close the door!"

Buchanan pulled the door to. Outside the two ladies were hooting with laughter.

A light came on revealing a man in his twenties with greasy hair and a goatee beard beside a woman around the same age, with short spiky red hair. The man held a blank piece of photographic paper and looked distraught.

"Man!" he moaned. "Have you never heard of knocking?"

"I'm sorry, I understood you were expecting me."

"Expecting you to come barging into my dark room and ruin the picture I was developing? Why would I expect something like that, man?"

"My name is Brant—"

"And my name's Frank," interrupted the man, "but what's that got to do with this non-knocking policy of yours?"

"Frank, dude, cool it," said the woman. "This is Brant Buchanan, the English guy I told you about. Pleased to meet you, Mr Buchanan, sir. Sorry about Frank. He gets tetchy. I'm Precious. I'm the one who spoke to your colleague. I'm really pleased to meet you."

"I'm sorry about your friend's picture. I didn't know anyone developed pictures these days."

Precious laughed. "Yeah, well, Frank likes to do things the old-fashioned way. I keep telling him to go digital."

"Was the Loch Ness monster caught on digital? Was Big Foot or the Roswell alien on digital? No, man, none of them were," said Frank, picking up a pile of photos from one of the messy workspaces that surrounded the room. He held out three blurry black-and-white pictures that Buchanan recognized as apparent sightings of unexplained things.

"That's because digital hadn't been invented then, dude," said Precious.

"Or had it?"

"Not this again." Precious sighed.

"It's what I believe, man," said Frank.

"Not in front of guests," insisted Precious. "Remember, we have a rule."

Frank hesitated.

"No, please, I'm an open-minded man," said

Buchanan. "That is why I'm here after all. Say whatever you have to say."

"See, *he's* open-minded," said Frank.

Precious sighed again.

"I believe that digital photography was created in order to stop us from finding out the truth," said Frank. "Unlike old-fashioned technology it was created by – and is now being controlled by – super-intelligent aliens that live right here on Earth with us, man." He whispered this as though fearful that someone might be listening.

"And where are these aliens?" asked Mr Buchanan.

"They're all around us." Frank lowered his voice to a whisper. "They're cats, man. You should see the way they look at me. They know I know."

"Frank, dude," interrupted Precious. "You sound crazy when you talk like that."

Brant Buchanan began to edge towards the door. "I'm sorry, I think I've made a mistake."

"No, man, don't go," said Precious. "It's just Frank. He's perfectly fine except for the alien cats thing. Frank, you should keep that stuff for your movie scripts. You want to know about dragons, don't you?"

"Let me make myself clear," said Mr Buchanan. "I have recently become interested in dragons. I don't care about aliens or vampires or things that go bump in the night. I'm not interested in any conspiracy theories on how the government covers things up because, believe me, no government in the world has any secrets from me. But a man in my position can't afford to let anyone find out that I'm in business with people such as yourselves. My stock would plummet. We live in a world of non-believers, my friends. People would think I had lost my mind if they thought I believed in dragons. Help me gather information discreetly and you will be handsomely rewarded."

Frank placed the photos down. "Yeah, well, I could be wrong about the cats, I suppose," he said.

"You want stuff on dragons?" said Precious.

"Yes, I want stuff on dragons," replied Buchanan.

PROD

8

DIR

CAM

None of this felt real to Holly. They had been driven to Heathrow airport, where, without delays or queues, they boarded a luxury private jet. It wasn't like any plane she had ever been on. After take-off, Holly and Archie spent the first couple of hours running around the plane, looking at all the cool stuff. When Holly's stepmum told them to sit still, they played computer games and watched films.

As Holly scrolled through the selection, she found one about dragons. She watched the first five minutes, but it was hard to take it seriously now she knew that dragons were real and nothing like how they were portrayed in movies. She missed Dirk. There was a phone on the plane but it was too risky, so she decided to call him when they arrived instead.

When the plane landed, there was no messing about with customs or passports. They simply went straight through to the car park where a black stretch limo was awaiting them.

"You'll be staying in the Hollywood Hills," said Weaver, their driver.

"Where they make all the films?" said Holly.

"You won't be far from the major studios," he replied matter-of-factly.

Mrs Bigsby could barely contain herself. "Wow, this is real star treatment," she enthused.

The limo took them to the city, where Holly was surprised to see that, in spite of the palm trees that lined the roads, large parts actually looked quite ordinary and grubby. It wasn't how she had imagined it at all. They headed up a winding road where the houses were bigger and much more how Holly had imagined they would look. Finally, they came to a set of gates, which opened automatically. At the end of the driveway was a large white house with columns along the front and an upstairs balcony.

When the car stopped Holly and Archie burst out

and ran to the house. It looked like part of a film set. It was too spotless and perfect to be a real house. Weaver opened the front door. Inside, a central staircase led to a landing and four large rooms, all of which had doors that opened on to the balcony.

Archie pushed one wide open and stepped out. The vast city lay before them, bathed in the soft early morning light.

"Nice view," he said.

"Try over here," replied Holly. She was standing at the corner of the balcony, looking the other way, up the hill. Archie joined her and saw what she was looking at.

Above them were nine giant letters, set in the hills, that spelled HOLLYWOOD.

"I imagine this sort of thing happens to you all the time," said Archie.

"Oh, every day," replied Holly.

"I may have to call my agent about my latest role," said Archie.

"Me too, I need a much bigger part," said Holly.

"Hey, I wonder if we're next door to anyone famous."

They tried to see into next door's garden but the houses were designed so you couldn't see in from the balcony. Archie suggested they try looking from one of the trees next to the fence.

As they ran downstairs into the garden, they passed Mrs Bigsby who shouted, "Stop running around, this isn't a playground!" Ignoring her, Holly and Archie found a climbable tree in the garden and went up.

Next door looked more like a fairy-tale castle than a house. It had turrets and cherub-like gargoyles and it was painted bright pink. The patio door was open and a girl's voice cut through the air.

"I don't care what anyone else says," said the girl. "My mum's exec-producing this film and she agrees with me. We need to reshoot the birth scene with me playing myself…"

"Who do you think it is?" whispered Archie.

Holly knew exactly who it was. The patio door opened and Petal Moses stepped out. She was sporting a pink tracksuit and holding the phone to her ear.

"Yes, I realize I would have been a baby, but I'm not having some other actor, baby or not, stealing my first

48

scene… I'll be playing myself… Of course, I know I don't look like a baby…" she yelled. "That's why they call it acting, darling. Besides, Mum says there's new technology where they can make me look like a baby if necessary… Chase says it's fine… Chase Lampton, the director, sweetie… Look, just drop the baby and let me know when I'm needed for the scene. OK?" She switched off the phone and shook her head in frustration. "Casting directors," she exclaimed, "what a nightmare."

"Morning, Petal," called Holly cheerfully.

Petal turned to see Holly halfway up the tree.

"You!" she said. "What are you doing here spying on me? I could have you arrested for invading my privacy."

"We're your new neighbours. This is Archie."

"Hello," said Archie, waving.

"But that house belongs to Brant Buchanan," said Petal sharply.

"Yes, my stepmum works for him," said Holly.

"I see. He's one of the investors in my film," said Petal, smiling smugly. "It's based on my book but we've made a few changes, you know, brought it up to date. It's still all about me, of course."

"Is it a comedy?" asked Archie.

"No," replied Petal. "It's a heart-warming tale of one very special girl's struggle to grow up under the harsh media spotlight."

"Sounds like a horror," said Holly.

"You don't know anything about movies. Chase says I've really got something."

"So long as you don't give it to us," said Holly.

Before Petal could think of a retort, a woman's voice called, "Petal Moses, come and have some breakfast before piano practice. And I don't want to hear any more excuses about learning lines. I promised your mother I would make you musical, which is proving to be more difficult than trying to teach algebra to an orangutan."

"Miss Gilfeather?" said Holly in amazement.

The severe-looking music teacher from William Scrivener School stepped out on to the patio holding a bowl of fruit and a glass of juice. Her auburn hair was hidden under a green beret. In spite of the strict tone she had taken with Petal she seemed more relaxed than when Holly had known her at school.

50

Following Petal's gaze, she looked up at the tree and saw Holly and Archie.

"Holly Bigsby, third trumpet," she said. "I hope you're still practising every day."

"Yes, Miss Gilfeather," lied Holly, who hadn't picked up her trumpet for weeks.

"Such a shame you had to leave us," said Miss Gilfeather warmly. "You did show a little potential, unlike some students." She looked at Petal.

"How dare you!" exclaimed Petal. "Employing you was the biggest mistake my mother ever made. As soon as she gets out of the studio, I'll make sure she fires you."

"Your mother employed me because she disagrees with me regarding your utter inability in the realms of music. She wants you to have the opportunity that she never had, to learn properly how to play an instrument."

"Have you been here all summer?" said Holly in disbelief, remembering how much disdain Miss Gilfeather had always showed for both Petal and her popstar mother.

Miss Gilfeather looked uncomfortable. "Well,

yes… I did have some misgivings when she asked but opportunities like this don't come along every day. I'd never been to this part of America before and I have to admit that popstars pay rather better than schools…"

The phone started to ring.

"Excuse me," said Petal. "Chase Lampton, the legendary director, is calling me." She picked up the phone and said, "Oh, Chase, darling, are you coming round?'"

"Why don't you join us for breakfast?" said Miss Gilfeather. "There's plenty of food and I could do with some civilized conversation for a change."

"Is that OK? And Archie too?" said Holly, who could hear Petal twittering on inside the house.

"Oh, yes," said Miss Gilfeather. "As much as it annoys madam, her mother put me in charge of the house while she's away recording her new album. Come over and I'll make some pancakes."

PROD

9

DIR

CAM

"Where are you going?" demanded Mrs Bigsby as Holly and Archie made for the front door.

"We've been invited next door for breakfast. Miss Gilfeather is staying there."

"Your old music teacher?" said her dad.

"What a small world it is. I wouldn't want to decorate it though," added her stepmum, laughing at her own joke.

Archie and Holly looked at each other. America appeared to have had a rather odd effect on Holly's parents. They were both more excited and animated than usual and there was, so far, no sign of this urgent business that Mrs Bigsby had been brought over to deal with.

"So it's OK to go round?" said Holly.

"Of course. Don't be too long, I thought we'd go and see the sights later on," said her dad.

Holly and Archie headed down the drive.

"I think the sun's gone to their heads," said Archie, looking up at the perfect blue sky.

Holly pressed the buzzer outside Petal's house and the gate opened. They headed up the driveway and Miss Gilfeather welcomed them into the house. The walls were covered with framed discs, album artwork and photos from Petal's mum's career. A cabinet by the door displayed hundreds of gleaming awards in different shapes and sizes. In the centre of the hallway, at the base of the sweeping staircase, was a life-sized marble statue of Petal's mother kneeling in a puddle. Water trickled down from the statue's eyes and at the base of the statue was a gold plaque that read: *She weeps for world peace.*

"Apparently it's the name of one of her albums," said Miss Gilfeather. "Isn't it hideous?"

The buzzer sounded and Petal appeared at the top of the stairs.

"Will you get that, Miss Gilfeather? It'll be

Chase..." She stopped, noticing Holly and Archie. "What are you doing here?"

"I invited them round. And I am not your servant, Petal," said Miss Gilfeather, pressing the button to open the gate.

"You can't go inviting people to my house."

"As you well know, I am in charge in your mother's absence," said Miss Gilfeather. "Holly did, at least, show some glimmer of natural ability at the trumpet. Do you play anything?" she asked Archie.

"My dad gave me a guitar once," replied Archie.

"A lovely instrument if played well," said Miss Gilfeather approvingly.

"But the strings hurt my fingers too much," he added.

"Learning any instrument involves an element of pain to begin with," said the music teacher. "More often for those having to listen to the beginner's efforts, but one must go through the pain barrier in order to achieve beauty."

"Then what pain did you go through to achieve such captivating charm?" said a man, entering the hallway. He had thick, curly black hair and was wearing an expensive pair of sunglasses.

"Good morning, Mr Lampton," said Miss Gilfeather. "Is it too bright for you in here?"

The man smiled and removed his sunglasses to reveal dark brown eyes. "Hi, Vivian," he replied in a cool American accent. "And, please, it's Chase to my friends."

"Until we become friends I will stick with Mr Lampton, Mr Lampton. I'll make some coffee."

"Hi, Chase," Petal said, beaming and suddenly developing an American twang in her voice.

"And how is my talented leading lady?"

"I'm fine, thanks, Chase. Where's Dante?"

"He's on the phone to his agent. He'll be here in a minute. I see you've got guests this morning." Chase nodded at Holly and Archie. "I hope you two aren't distracting our star here."

"Oh, just ignore them," said Petal. "They aren't anybody."

"That's right, we're nobody," said Holly.

"I used to be somebody, but now I'm not anybody," said Archie.

Chase smiled and said to Petal, "Did you manage

to get a chance to look through the rewrite for the final scene?"

"Yes, I've made a few notes. I was thinking what if … wait for it … what if I were to fly at the end of the film?"

"Fly?" said Chase.

"Yes, what do you think? Mum thinks it would be a great way to end the film."

Chase paused as if visualizing the idea, then nodded. "Yeah, I can see that working. You could fly right over all the teachers and pupils in the concert. Real feel-good moment. Great idea."

"It ends with a concert?" said Holly.

"That's right," said Chase. "Petal's big moment when she sang her first solo at the school concert this year. It's not in the book but we thought it would make a good ending for the movie. We're filming it today. Why don't you come down and sit in the audience? It would be good to get some genuine Brit accents."

"I think you'll find mine to be a genuine British accent, Papa," said a boy who entered behind Chase. He had the same thick black hair and sunglasses as the director and he spoke with the least convincing accent Holly had ever heard.

"Hi, Dante," said Petal.

"Good morrow, dear lady," said Dante.

Holly and Archie fell about laughing.

"What's so funny?" he asked, reverting to his usual American voice.

"Nothing," said Archie. "I thought it was a splendid accent, old bean."

"Hey, thanks," said Dante, failing to notice that Archie was very clearly being sarcastic. "I'm Dante Lampton. I play Callum Thackley, the troubled but musically brilliant son of the Prime Minister."

"He's not *that* musically brilliant," said Petal.

"Callum's in the film?" replied Holly, astonished.

"It's only a supporting role," added Petal.

"I wanted to use the character of Callum to show how people deal with things differently," said Chase.

"Callum's not a character. He's a real person," protested Holly.

"What interests me is how the same kind of media attention that Petal thrives upon is what drove poor Callum … well, you know…" said Chase.

"That's not fair," said Holly, but she could hardly explain how the monsters that haunted Callum were not figments of his imagination but very real dragons.

"Oh yes, I forgot Holly had a crush on Callum," said Petal.

"I did not," said Holly. "We just played in the band together."

"So you were at the concert too?" said Chase. "Tell me what you can remember about it. We're recreating it today but there's no footage of it."

Holly could remember every detail of the horrific night when the evil Mountain Dragon Vainclaw Grandin had entranced the audience with Dragonsong, but she lied and said, "I only remember how good it was."

"Ha! You see," said Chase, snapping his fingers, "that's what everyone says. It's kind of spooky. You know, there are rumours online that something strange happened that night – like something, you know, magic."

"What nonsense. Unless you are referring to the magic of music," said Miss Gilfeather, stepping into the hallway, not realizing how close to the truth she was. After all, it was Dirk's Dragonsong that had caused everyone to forget the evening.

Chase smiled. "You know, Vivian, it's not too late to play yourself. The actress playing you isn't a patch on the real thing."

"I'm sure she would be flattered to hear you say so," replied Miss Gilfeather. "I'll be quite content as a member of the audience."

"Can we sit with you?" said Holly.

"Of course," said Miss Gilfeather. "Now come along. Breakfast is ready in the dining room."

The buzzer sounded again.

"You go ahead," said Chase. "That'll be my assistant, Tara. I'll be there in a minute."

In the dining room, Dante said, "So, Holly and Archie, do you want to be in the movies too?"

"No, when I grow up I'm going to be a detective," replied Holly, picturing herself sitting in an office like Dirk's or wearing a wide-brimmed hat like Ladbroke Blake, a human detective she knew who had once been hired to follow her and had, ever since, helped her out of some tight spots.

"Since you know Callum, can you tell me what you

60

think of my performance?" said Dante. "I've not been able to meet him but I really want to understand what makes him tick. It's the key to great acting, you know. A great actor has to understand what drives each character."

Again, Holly was reminded that Callum's biggest driving factor was the strange connection he had formed with an evil dragon intent on waging war on the human world.

They sat down at the table and helped themselves to the breakfast Miss Gilfeather had laid out.

In the hallway they could hear someone talking loudly.

"Chase, I don't know where to start… The whole thing's unbelievable…"

"Calm down, Tara," said Chase. "Let's go and get something to eat. I need a coffee."

A young woman with dark curly hair entered the room with Chase, waving her arms in the air and moving agitatedly. Chase poured himself a coffee and sat down. "Now what is it?" he said.

Tara was fidgeting so much she didn't look like she was capable of sitting down. She took a deep breath.

"We were filming in the desert—"

"Why do we need a boring old desert in the film?" asked Petal.

"It's for the opening sequence. It's symbolic, you know, representing a cultural desert, isolation … that kind of thing," said Chase.

"Oh, that sounds very clever." Petal addressed Holly. "Chase is old school. He's making the entire picture on actual film."

"Yes, and it's causing me nightmares," said Tara. "Do you know how hard – and expensive – it is to get film digitised in this town?"

"I don't need to," said Chase. "That's why I have you. And using film adds authenticity to my pictures."

"Yeah, well," continued Tara. "We got lots of nice shots using the long-angle lens. We went early morning and just where you said, two miles down the road from the southern entrance to Joshua Tree National Park. You were right, the light's real nice at dawn, it made for pretty shots. The sun was coming up and the desert had a kind of reddish glow."

"Sounds beautiful," said Chase, stirring cream into his coffee.

"Then…" Tara faltered. "Then something got in the way of the shot."

"What sort of something?"

"Something big. It was in the distance but you could see what it was. There were two of them. I looked back at the film to check."

"Well," said Chase patiently. "What was it? A roadrunner? A wolf? There's not much that lives out there."

"It wasn't any of those things," said Tara. "It was… Well, it looked like… You know, from a distance it seemed to be…"

"Spit it out," said Chase. "I haven't got all day."

"D-d-dragons," she whispered.

Petal and Dante hooted with laughter.

A smile spread across Chase's face.

Holly and Archie said nothing.

"I think you may have got the wrong idea about the sort of movie we're making," said Chase, sipping his coffee.

"Look, I know how it sounds but I know what I saw and I saw dragons. They looked like those Joshua trees you get out there – you know, all spiky like cactuses, but they had jaws and limbs and they were fighting."

"How ridiculous," said Petal scornfully. "Dragons don't exist in real life, do they, Chase?"

"Not in my experience," replied the director ponderously. "Look, Tara, I'll tell you what, let me see the rushes. I'd like to have a look at these dragons. It's probably just a trick of the light."

"That's the problem," said Tara. "The film's gone missing. It was stolen."

PROD

10

DIR
CAM

Dirk was in the middle of a dream about the moon being a huge orange, which had ripened and was on a collision course with Earth, when the phone rang.

"Someone get a juicer!" cried Dirk, waking up with a start. His mouth was parched and two empty bottles of orange squash lay on his desk. He groaned, knocked them on to the floor and answered the ringing phone.

"The Dragon Detective Agency," he said gruffly. "Dirk Dilly speaking. How can I help you?"

"Have you just woken up?" It was Holly. "What time is it there?"

"What do you mean *there*? Where are you?" said Dirk.

"I'm calling long distance," said Holly. "I'm in Los Angeles."

"Los Angeles in America?" spluttered Dirk.

"No, Los Angeles in Kuala Lumpur," said Holly, laughing.

"I thought you were grounded," said Dirk.

"We got flown here on Brant Buchanan's private jet."

"I don't trust your stepmum's boss as far as I could throw him. In fact, I don't trust him as far as he could throw me."

"Nor do I, but that's not why I'm calling. Have you ever heard of Chase Lampton?"

"The film director? Sure," said Dirk. "He directed one of my favourite films, *The Big Zero*. He hasn't made anything as good since but that one was a classic."

"Well, he's making a new film now, only one of the cameras caught something in the desert first thing this morning."

"What kind of something?"

"Dragons," said Holly.

"Rats in pyjamas!" exclaimed Dirk, sitting up. "This

is serious. Where's the film?"

"No one knows. It's been stolen."

"You were right to call. We can't let that film stay in human hands," said Dirk. "That evidence could be all over the internet by lunchtime. Then it's game over."

Dirk took down the phone number and address of where Holly was staying and committed them both to memory. Holly told him what she knew about where the film had been made, and then she told him about their amazing journey to America and how Chase had asked her and Archie to be in the film too.

After saying goodbye, Dirk put the receiver down, opened a desk drawer and pulled out Mrs Klingerflim's copy of *Dragonlore*, flicking to the chapter on Desert Dragons.

The Desert Dragon is different from other subspecies of dragon in that it spits a deadly poison rather than breathing fire. The poison is a potent acid that will cut through the strongest material, fell a mighty tree or kill any creature in seconds. However, Desert Dragons can only hold one dose of poison at a time, which takes them around twenty-four hours to produce. So, once the poison is used up, all you have to worry about are the teeth, claws and hundreds of spikes which cover their bodies.

Dirk placed the book back in the drawer and considered the best way to get to America. Flying, swimming or taking the lithosphere tunnel would take too long. If there was a possibility that the film was being watched by a human, he had to move fast. Dirk switched off the TV and headed downstairs.

He stopped outside the kitchen, where Mrs Klingerflim was clattering about preparing her dinner, humming along to some old crackly jazz that was coming from her tinny radio. She held down a button on top of her oven, creating the hiss of gas and a clicking noise, but failing to light the hob.

"Bother to this old thing," she exclaimed. "Oh, Mr Dilly, excuse my language. I didn't see you there."

"Let me help you with that," said Dirk.

She stood back. Dirk leaned over the hob and sent a tiny flicker of flame from between his two front teeth, lighting the hob. Mrs Klingerflim smiled and placed a pan of water on it.

"Thank you, Mr Dilly," she said. "Off out, are you?"

"I've got a case out of town so I wanted to let you know that the rent may be a little late and that I won't be around to help."

"Oh, don't worry about that," said the sweet old lady. "I've always got Mr Blandford. He pops round sometimes to help out. He put up these shelves."

"Sounds like you've got an admirer," said Dirk, winking.

"Oh, Mr Dilly, don't be daft," said Mrs Klingerflim, blushing and changing the subject. "Are you going anywhere nice?"

"California," replied Dirk.

Mrs Klingerflim smiled wistfully. "California. How lovely. I went there with Ivor once, you know. Stunning scenery."

"Dragon-spotting?" asked Dirk. All of Mrs Klingerflim's holidays with her late husband had been research for the book.

"Oh yes, those Californian Desert Dragons are very territorial but beautiful movers. I wouldn't want to get on the wrong side of one, though."

"I'll bear that in mind," he said. "No skydiving

while I'm away, Mrs K."

"Oh, I'll be too busy wrestling Welsh Rock Dragons," joked the frail old lady. "How are you getting there?"

"Smelding," replied Dirk.

"Oh, really? How interesting. Good luck."

Dirk left her and went down to the cellar, climbing into the hole Karnataka had made and clawing his way through the broken bits of concrete into the ground. Soon he reached the rock that lay beneath the foundations of the house.

In the dark, Dirk lay flat on the rock and concentrated on relaxing every muscle in his body. It wasn't easy but after a few minutes he felt a tingling pain on the soft skin of his belly and the underside of his neck and limbs.

In his book, Ivor Klingerflim described smelding like this:

> *The act of smelding is unique to Mountain Dragons and is an extension of blending. Only, rather than repositioning particles that form the colour of a surface over the dragon, it involves the dragon*

squeezing each particle of their body between the particles that form the rock beneath them. The process of reducing itself to formless particles takes the dragon around an hour but it means there is no resistance and they can choose to re-emerge anywhere in the world.

Dirk wasn't sure about the science of it but he did know that it hurt. The knack with smelding was to stay relaxed during the painful process, which felt like being eaten by a million tiny sharp-toothed fish. It was a technique developed during the Ice Age, when dragons had to travel thousands of miles to find edible vegetation. Dirk was grateful that he lived in more convenient times. It was bad enough when his supermarket got his order wrong and sent him the cheap tins of beans that were all sauce and no beans.

Eventually he felt himself smelding into the rock, his skin, bones and green blood slipping into the space in between the particles. Once fully immersed, it was an odd feeling. Without eyes, he couldn't see anything and without feet, he couldn't feel anything. He knew he still existed but, without a physical body, there was a lightness to his existence that was extremely relaxing. He had heard of dragons who had never reappeared after having smelded and Dirk could understand why. He fought the lethargy that swept over him and sensed a rock in the Californian Desert where he could begin the equally painful re-emergence.

By the time he felt sunlight on his face, Dirk was exhausted. He looked weakly at the scenery that was appearing in front of his newly formed eyes. A dusty, stony landscape stretched out in front of him as far as he could see. Strange, leafless trees with twisted branches were dotted around, each growing a metre or so apart. The thick branches were covered in light brown spikes with clumps of green spikes at the end. Dirk recognized them as Joshua trees from a nature programme he had seen once. Between them, dry shrubs struggled to find enough water to survive. All around were huge piles of boulders and rocks. The sky was pastel blue with only a couple of fluffy clouds to accompany the blazing sun. There wasn't a living creature in sight.

The final piece of Dirk's claws appeared and he passed out.

When Dirk awoke, the sun was high in the sky and every part of his body ached. Vowing to take a slower but easier route home, he stretched, jumped down from the rock and began searching for dragons. He checked the healthier shrubs, looking for nibble marks. He examined the ground for footprints. The problem with tracking dragons was that, unlike humans, they left very little indication of where they had been.

Dirk heard a noise. He stopped dead. Something had moved but all he could see were the strangely shaped Joshua trees. It was probably a desert rat or a wolf, but as a precaution he raised himself on to his hind legs and drew his claws, prepared to fight if necessary.

He remained perfectly still, listening for another sound. He turned around as something flew over him. A weight landed on his back. He stumbled forwards, tripped on a root and fell to the ground. Spikes dug into his skin, so sharp he could even feel them through the hard skin on his back. Dirk craned his neck just enough to catch a glimpse of the spiky face of a particularly vicious-looking Desert Dragon before it pushed his head to the ground. Strong limbs pinned him to the earth and a thin voice said, "You looking to rumble, dragon? You come trespessin' on my turf lookin' for a fight?"

"I surrender," said Dirk, hoping that the Desert Dragon on his back had already used up his day's worth of poison.

"That's real funny," said an incredulous voice. "You come struttin' into my territory, ready to rumble and you expect me to believe that you surrender? Old Putz ain't no klutz. You're a friend of Kitelsky's, ain't you? I shoulda saw it comin', a cheap trick like this. He don't wanna play fair no more."

"Listen, Putz, my name's Dirk Dilly. I'm a detective. I didn't come here to fight and I don't know anyone called Kitelsky," said Dirk.

"Dirk Dilly? What kind of silly name is that?"

"It's my name," snarled Dirk, "and don't call me silly."

"You don't get to give orders on my turf, OK, particularly when I found you with your claws ready flicked," said Putz.

"I only drew my claws because I heard a noise," said Dirk.

"A noise? I didn't make no noise. Old Putz is a silent assailant."

"Sure you made a noise," said another voice.

"Kitelsky," growled Putz. "I knew it. So he *is* with you."

At first it looked to Dirk like one of the Joshua trees was moving, but what Dirk had taken for branches were thick limbs. What had looked like a mound of dead grass at the foot of the tree was a dragon's head, with two yellow eyes set in the middle. A tail swung into view, with a cone of white spikes at the end.

"He ain't with me," said Kitelsky. "It looks to me like he's with you."

"If he were with me, why would I be pinning him down, which I am doing, I should say, with no small degree of ease and expertise?" replied Putz.

"Because that's how you treat your friends, Putz," replied Kitelsky bitterly.

Dirk felt the weight lift from his back as Putz flew at Kitelsky, his spikes splayed out, but Kitelsky was ready for him, diving out of the way, leaving Putz to land into a roll before jumping back on to all fours and squaring off.

Putz's skin was lighter than Kitelsky's, with sharp green spikes on the end of his tail and, where Kitelsky had a grassy beard, Putz's craggy chin was visible. He snarled, showing his white teeth.

Maintaining eye contact, the two dragons started to sway, head to head, moving slowly in a circle. A bubbling noise came from the backs of their throats. Dirk edged away.

As they paced, he understood what Mrs Klingerflim had meant about their movements being beautiful. They stepped in perfect time with each other. It was like watching a graceful dance.

Then Putz broke step. He opened his mouth wide and spat a stream of luminous green liquid at the other dragon. Kitelsky ducked and the liquid flew over his head, hitting the tree behind him, which hissed as the poison burned straight through its bark and caused it to fall to the ground.

Neither Desert Dragon looked at the tree, their yellow eyes remaining fixed on each other. They were now moving back and forth, mirroring each other's movements. Kitelsky took a side-step, then spat poison at Putz. Putz jumped into the air to avoid it, somersaulting over Kitelsky, who spun round, bringing them face to face again.

"You're trespassin' on my turf," said Putz.

"This ain't your territory and you know it," replied Kitelsky.

"I'm claimin' it," said Putz.

"You gotta earn it first."

"Let's rumble then."

The two dragons went at each other with claws, teeth and spikes. As vicious as it looked, it seemed to Dirk that they knew each other's moves so well that they barely made contact. It looked more like an elaborate routine than a real fight.

After a while the two dragons began to tire.

"Your Mountain Dragon ain't gettin' involved then," said Putz, standing back.

"I told you, he ain't with me," replied Kitelsky.

"Well, he ain't with me either," said Putz.

They both turned to look at Dirk.

"You only get one dose of poison a day," said Dirk, who had been ready for this. "I get fire twenty-four-seven." He sent flames billowing forwards, setting the fallen branch on fire. The Desert Dragons jumped back from the burning tree.

"You fire spitters are all the same," said Putz. "You think you're so much better than us. It still don't change the fact that you're trespassin' on my turf."

"Putz, this is Mo's turf," said Kitelsky. "And you're only jealous. Putz is always trying to breathe fire."

"No I ain't," said Putz.

"You're pathetic," said Kitelsky.

"Are there any other dragons in the area?" asked Dirk.

"Not since Mo left, no," said Kitelsky. "Just us two. Why?"

"Where were you at dawn this morning?" asked Dirk.

"We were scufflin'," said Kitelsky.

"What's that mean?"

"It's when you fight for your territory," said Putz. "You beat a dragon in a scuffle and you get their turf.

We do it at sunrise and sunset on the borders of our territory."

"Yeah and you never beaten Mo, so this ain't your turf," said Kitelsky.

"Only cos Mo ain't here to scuffle with me," said Putz, squaring up for another fight.

"I'm not interested in your territorial disputes," said Dirk, sending another blast of fire into the air as a warning.

"What do you want then?" said Kitelsky.

"Two dragons were caught on camera this morning," said Dirk. "You know what a camera is, I take it?"

"Of course we do," said Kitelsky. "You can't live in California without knowing about cameras."

"That's right," said Putz. "We ain't stupid."

"Then you'll know that the punishment for being seen by a human is banishment to the Inner Core," said Dirk.

"The Inner Core?" The colour drained from Putz's face.

"What's it to you, anyway, Dilly?" said Kitelsky. "You come here saying we done this and that. We

80

don't even know you."

"You know what?" snapped Dirk angrily. "You're right, I should leave you to it. I was going to find and destroy the tape, but now I might just go home and crack open a fresh bottle of squash in front of a good movie instead."

"Hey, don't be so hasty," said Putz. "Kitelsky don't mean to disrespect you or nothin'. Do you, Kitelsky?"

"I don't trust him," said Kitelsky. "How do we know he ain't gonna do the dirty on us?"

"I haven't got time for this. I'm going to retrieve that tape and save your spiky necks," said Dirk, turning to leave. He could tell that the Desert Dragons didn't know any more than they were letting on. He was wasting his time.

"Where you going?" said Kitelsky.

"Los Angeles," replied Dirk.

"We're comin' with you," said Kitelsky.

"Are you outta your mind, Kitelsky?" said Putz. "I ain't goin' to no human city."

"You stay here then," replied Kitelsky. "I don't trust this Mountain Dragon."

"I work alone," said Dirk.

"Did I say I was givin' you the choice?" said Kitelsky. "If there's a film showin' me and Putz, I ain't gonna sit around and leave it to no out-of-town detective to sort out."

"I'm goin' if you're goin'," said Putz.

"And what do you know about city life?" said Dirk.

"That ain't the point. Like it or not, we're comin' wi' you," said Kitelsky.

12

"This is weird," said Archie, reaching into his pocket and pulling out a jellybean.

"It's really weird," agreed Holly.

They were sitting on wooden chairs in the front row of an exact replica of Little Hope Village Hall where Holly's school concert had taken place. The fake hall was perfect down to the finest detail except for one of the walls being missing, revealing that they were actually inside a huge hanger in World Studios. Where the wall should have been were cameras and hundreds of people who bustled around with clipboards and expensive-looking equipment. Chase Lampton sat in a director's chair wearing his sunglasses and a look of frustration.

During the eleven takes so far Petal hadn't even come close to remembering the words to the dreary song her mother had written for the grand finale of the film.

To keep everyone occupied between takes Tara was telling the band members their character names in case it helped them get into their parts.

Holly, Archie and Miss Gilfeather were in the audience, so they didn't have character names.

"On third trumpet we have Holly Bigsby," said Tara, pointing at a blond girl with exceptionally white teeth.

"Not an exact likeness, is it?" said Miss Gilfeather under her breath.

"So is yours," said Holly, pointing to the beautiful young actress playing Miss Gilfeather, waving a baton around.

"What does that woman think she's doing?" said Miss Gilfeather.

"Looks like she's sword-fighting the Invisible Man," said Archie.

Miss Gilfeather allowed herself a tiny smile. "It's certainly not conducting," she said. "That young lady couldn't conduct a survey on whether monkeys like bananas. And as for that Lampton boy, he looks like he's never seen a French horn before."

Dante Lampton was sitting at the front of the stage, in character as Callum Thackley, holding the instrument upside down.

"OK, everybody." Chase spoke through a loudhailer. "We're ready for another take. Petal Moses to set, please."

Petal Moses arrived in one of the little white buggies used to shuttle the more important cast members to and from the VIP area. She got off the buggy and drifted on to the set, wearing an extremely sparkly dress. She took her place in front of the stage, then announced, "I'm ready."

"Quiet on set, please. *Petal: The Movie*, scene fifty-six, take twelve," shouted a man with a clapperboard.

The lights dimmed and the music began.

"Excellent, I love this tune," said Archie, forcing Holly to stifle her giggles.

"Don't make me laugh," she said. "I need the loo."

"I bet you a jellybean she messes up again," whispered Archie.

"Be quiet," scolded Miss Gilfeather. "We'll only have to hear it again."

"All she has to do is mime along with herself. How difficult can it be?" said Holly under her breath.

As if in answer to her question, Chase shouted, "Cut!"

"Anything wrong, Chase, darling?" asked Petal sweetly.

"Petal, remember what we said about moving your mouth in time with the words," replied the director.

"I'm sorry, Chase. I keep forgetting where I come in."

"You've got four bars, then the twiddly piano bit, then you come in," said Chase.

"Oh yes. Sorry, Chase."

"That's fine," said Chase patiently.

"Dad, can I ask something?" said Dante.

"Sure thing, son," replied Chase.

"I was thinking that my character would be fairly conflicted here, you know, pleased that he is in the concert but bitter that Petal's getting the limelight, like both happy and unhappy at the same time. Like this." Dante pulled a face.

"He looks more like he's constipated and got diarrhoea at the same time," said Archie.

Holly shook with laughter. "Stop it! I really need the loo," she said.

"That's perfect, son," said Chase. "OK, let's take a fifteen-minute break, then we'll go for it one more time."

"Great, I'm going to the toilet," said Holly.

"I'd hurry. I don't think you're the only one with that idea," said Miss Gilfeather, pointing at the swarm of people heading in the same direction. Holly and Archie tried to get through, but the crowd was bottle-necking at the door by the stage.

Holly's heart sank when she saw that there was already a long queue coming from the toilet. "I'm bursting," she moaned.

"Hi, guys," said Dante, as he passed them on one of the electric buggies, sitting next to his dad.

"I'll bet *they* don't have to queue for the toilet," said Archie.

"I know, but you need one of those passes," replied Holly, watching as the buggy reached a doorway and a security guard checked their passes and waved them through.

"If only you could turn invisible," said Archie, with a wide grin. "Oh, hold on… You can."

Holly smiled, then said, "What about you?"

"I'll be fine – the queue isn't as long for the boys. I'll cause a diversion for you. Look, there's Tara." Archie ran over to her, jumping in front of the buggy she was driving.

"Excuse me," he said.

Tara slammed her foot on the brake. "Hey, be careful!" she cried.

"Sorry, but I've been meaning to ask how you got to become an assistant director."

Tara beamed at Archie. "The first thing you need is a love of film," she said. "From a very young age I've always loved movies. But that's not enough. You have to be willing to work hard. The hours are long but in the end…"

While she spoke, Holly snuck round the side of the buggy, checked no one was looking and climbed on. Tara must have caught a glimpse of her in the corner of her eye because she broke off what he was saying to glance back, but Holly had vanished.

"Thanks for the advice," said Archie.

"No problem. Nice talking to you." Tara handed him her business card and started the buggy again, unaware of her invisible passenger.

The buggy drove briefly into the bright sunshine, across the tarmac to another hanger, where there were a few office desks, a coffee bar and, Holly was pleased to see, a row of toilets with no queue.

Tara parked and went to get a coffee. Holly checked no one was looking and ran to the toilet.

With her bladder finally relieved she went back to Tara's buggy, climbed on and blended into the seat, waiting for Tara to take her back.

She had been waiting for a minute, watching Tara attempt to drink her coffee without getting her nose covered in froth, when she saw Chase and Dante Lampton walking over to where she was hiding. Chase had an arm round Dante's shoulder. For a moment she was worried that they were going to sit on her, but they remained standing.

"… but that's not fair," Dante was saying. He seemed upset.

"You gotta toughen up if you want to make it in

this industry," replied his father.

"But I worked so hard on this role. I really feel like I got a hook on this character."

"I know," said Chase, who didn't look like he was enjoying the conversation any more than Dante was. "You've done some great work on it but Callum was always only a small part. The film's about Petal."

"But you're talking about cutting half of my scenes," said Dante.

"Keep your voice down," hissed Chase. "Listen, I'm doing this for your own good."

"How can it be for my own good to cut my part out of the film?"

"Son, I'm only going to say this once and I don't want you to repeat it but the fact is…" He lowered his voice even more. "The fact is … this is a lousy film."

Dante stared in disbelief at what he was being told.

"I hoped it would be OK," Chase continued. "A kind of fun film about celebrity culture. But it's not. It's dross. It's garbage. I've been watching the rushes and there's no saving it. Every time I try to make it better, that girl comes along with some stupid idea to make it worse."

"But you're the director," said Dante.

"And her mum's the exec producer. I have to go along with it."

"Isn't there anything that can be done?" asked Dante.

"Yes, I can save you," said his father. "The fact is that this is going to be the worst film of my career. I'll probably never direct again. It's going to stink so bad that anyone associated with it is going to carry the stench, me included. I don't want your career being damaged. That's why I'm cutting your role. OK?"

Dante took all this in, then said, "Thanks, Dad. I love you." He hugged his father.

"I love you too, son," said Chase.

"How sweet," said Petal Moses, whose driver brought her buggy alongside them. "Hold on, Mum," she said into the phone she was holding to her ear. "Chase is here now. Hi, Chase. Mum says that it doesn't matter if I mime out of time with the music because you'll be able to sort it out in the edit."

"That's actually not so easy, Petal," said Chase patiently.

"He says it's not that easy," she said into the phone. "Yes, I'll tell him." She looked at him again. "Mum says it *is* that easy and don't be so lazy, Chase, darling."

Chase smiled. "Sure thing, Petal. It's not a problem."

PROD

13

DIR
CAM

Dirk Dilly wasn't easily impressed, but standing on the Y of the Hollywood sign in the hills above Los Angeles, he couldn't help admiring the view. It was early evening. The city lights stretched on for miles, reminding Dirk of the opening sequence to *The Big Zero*.

"Get yourself off that thing," said Kitelsky, poking his head round the side of the W.

"Yeah, you get seen, we're all in trouble," said Putz, looking through a huge O.

Dirk had noticed that, as the two Desert Dragons got nearer the city, they had become increasingly nervous about being spotted.

"Right, let's get going," he said, jumping down.

"What? Now?" said Kitelsky.

"Maybe we should get a good night's sleep first," said Putz.

"Whoever's stolen that film won't be sleeping," said Dirk. "Besides, it'll be easier to travel across the roofs at night."

"Across the roofs?" said Putz.

"Of course," said Dirk casually. "Don't worry, city-dwelling humans don't look up much and most of them here seem to be in cars."

"But what if one of them does look up?" said Putz.

"If you get spotted just stop and blend," said Dirk. "Humans are easily distracted. A song will come on the radio that they like, or they'll see something in a shop window, or they'll catch a whiff from a fast food restaurant and the memory of the shadow that passed overhead will vanish like that." Dirk clicked his claws together and jumped on to an L.

"Blend? What you talking about?" said Putz. "Desert Dragons can't blend."

"Really? I didn't know that," said Dirk innocently.

"You know full well that only Mountain Dragons can blend," said Kitelsky.

"Then you'll just have to take your chances. Unless…" Dirk paused.

"Unless what?" said Kitelsky.

"No, forget it," replied Dirk.

"Unless what, Dilly?" repeated Kitelsky.

"Look, you two are quick but you don't know this environment. Me, I'm an urban-based Mountain Dragon. Why don't you stay here and keep look out? I'll go find the tape and bring it back."

"No way," said Kitelsky. "We're comin' with you."

"Fair enough," said Dirk, heading down the hill. "Just remember to keep away from convertibles… Oh, and watch out for window cleaners … and all those tall buildings in the financial area could cause a problem … and don't forget roof gardens…"

"Gee, Kitelsky," said Putz. "You know what he's talking about?"

"It seems to me like this Mountain Dragon spends a lot of time around humans," replied Kitelsky.

"Maybe we should leave it to him," said Putz.

"I'm inclined to agree with you," said Kitelsky.

"You're not coming?" said Dirk.

"Don't look so pleased," said Kitelsky. "We'll be

here, cooking up some fresh poison that's comin' your way if I smell so much as a whiff of double-crossin'."

"Fine," said Dirk.

"We'll wait here by the sign," said Putz.

"You'd better come and tell us when you find somethin'," said Kitelsky.

"You have my word."

Dirk headed down the hill, where the trees got thicker and provided enough cover to move swiftly to the city. He found an empty phone box in a quiet street. Checking the coast was clear, he jumped down to it, grabbed the receiver, prized open the bottom, took out a coin and dropped it into the slot to make the call.

"Hello?" said Holly.

"Hey, kiddo, it's me."

"Dirk!" she exclaimed. "Where are you?"

"Same city as you," said Dirk.

"You're in LA?" said Holly.

"LA? Listen to you, you've gone all showbiz on me. How was your big film role?"

"It was strange." She told him about the scene in Little Hope Village Hall, then she said, "How about you? Any clues about the film yet?"

"I've found the stars, a couple of Desert Dragons from out of town. A right pair of characters, not too friendly, but they didn't seem to know anything about the filming."

"So what's next?" asked Holly.

"Any ideas who the last person to see the film was?" asked Dirk.

"That would have been the assistant, Tara," replied Holly.

"Any other details?"

"Archie, Dirk's on the phone. Give me that card Tara gave you," said Holly. "Thanks. Tara Leggett, assistant director." She read out a phone number.

"Holly and Archie, come down here immediately," shouted Holly's dad. "We have dinner reservations."

"Coming," shouted Holly. "You don't think Buchanan's involved in this, do you?"

"We've got no reason to suspect him," said Dirk.

"I suppose not," said Holly. "Archie says hi."

"Hi to Archie," replied Dirk. "If the trail leads to Buchanan, I'll let you know, but I'm going to start with this Tara character. Nine times out of ten in my experience the last person to see something is the first person you should suspect of having taken it. I'll speak soon."

Dirk hung up, then used the same coin to make another call to Tara's number. It rang once, then a female voice answered. "Tara Leggett speaking. Hello?"

"Ms Leggett, my name's Dirk Dilly. I work for an insurance company," said Dirk, doing his best to sound professional. "I need to ask you a few questions."

"What insurance company?" There was a note of suspicion in her voice.

"Holly Insurance," replied Dirk, improvising as he went along. "Holly of Hollywood. We cover World Studios. I understand a tape went missing this morning."

"I've never heard of you. Who is this?" demanded Tara.

"I told you, I'm—"

"Don't give me a story about an insurance company. I already spoke to the studio insurance people. He's put you up to this, hasn't he? Well, I told him that I don't know who took the film and that's what I'm telling you. And I've never heard of anyone called Sorrentino. Now leave me alone."

The phone went dead.

The sun was setting and the sky was turning mauve. Dirk felt a wave of exhaustion sweep over him. All in all it had been a long day. He decided to return to the hill for the night, then make an early start in the morning. He bounded up the hill, through the trees and had reached the Hollywood sign when a thorny weight landed on his back.

"Where you goin', Dilly?" said Kitelsky, his spikes digging into Dirk's back.

"Get off me," growled Dirk. "How many times do I have to say it? I'm trying to help," said Dirk. "Where's Putz?"

Kitelsky released Dirk. "He's down the hill actin' a fool. Come on, I'll show you," he said, walking into the trees.

Dirk opened his mouth and shot fire at Kitelsky's backside.

"Ow! What did you go doin' that for?" said Kitelsky.

"That's a reminder not to go jumping on me again," said Dirk.

They found Putz standing in a clearing, carefully patting down a mound of old newspapers. He stood back, took aim, closed his eyes and blew. Bits of newspaper went flying everywhere.

"What's he doing?" asked Dirk.

"Tryin' to breathe fire," replied Kitelsky, with an amused smirk.

Torn pages of newspaper fluttered back down to the ground.

"If you can do it, I can do it," said Putz, seeing Dirk. "We're dragons, ain't we? We got wings and teeth and claws and green blood. Ain't no reason why we all can't breathe fire. Show me how you do it. I reckon I could learn easy."

Dirk grabbed a sheet of newspaper from the ground, rolled it up and exhaled a thin line of fire, instantly igniting it.

"Looks easy enough," said Putz, grabbing another couple of sheets and blowing on them. Instead of setting the paper on fire, he only managed to make it flap pathetically.

"I keep tellin' him that we ain't designed for fire-breathin'," said Kitelsky.

"Give me that," said Dirk, snatching the paper from Putz's paws.

"Hey, mind your claws," said Putz. "I reckon I got close that time. I could feel my throat gettin' kinda warm."

Dirk wasn't listening. He had opened the paper. It was a page of classified ads. At the bottom was an advert that read:

Sorrentino Solutions

If you've got a problem, we'll find the solution

14

Dirk, Kitelsky and Putz spent the night on the hill overlooking Los Angeles, taking turns to stay awake and keep watch for humans. Dirk took the first shift, then settled down by Kitelsky, leaving Putz on look-out duty.

It had been a long day and Dirk fell asleep instantly. He dreamed that he was in a film about St George and the Dragon, in which he was playing the knight opposite Brant Buchanan as the dragon. In the dream an unseen director kept shouting at Dirk for forgetting his one line, which was, "Die, dragon, die!"

When he woke up, the sky had turned a hazy yellow and the vast city was half hidden by heavy smog. Both Kitelsky and Putz were sleeping, curled up with their spikes on the outside, looking like two dense patches of cactuses.

Dirk yawned and picked up the piece of newspaper with the details of Sorrentino Solutions, then tiptoed away. Dirk preferred being on his own.

Although LA had initially felt a world apart from London, seen from the rooftops, it wasn't all that different. The fact that so many more people travelled by car than walked made it easier for Dirk to make his way to the address without being spotted.

Sorrentino Solutions was a small operation on the top floor of a downtown office block. From his position on the roof, Dirk could hear the secretary – whose name was Sandra – taking and making calls. Dirk couldn't hear the other side of the conversations but she received calls about a range of problems, which she would then inform her boss about. These varied from missing people, thefts, neighbourly grudges, vandalism and minor acts of revenge. There appeared to be no job this Sorrentino character wouldn't deal with. Dirk listened carefully until, towards the end of the day, his ears pricked up when Sandra revealed details of where he could find this mysterious problem-solver.

"You are to meet the contact on the top level of the parking lot by the Grove shopping complex in half an hour," she said.

Dirk had noticed the location on his trip across town and was there in no time at all. The top level of the car park was empty and the sun was setting. He found a good hiding spot behind a concrete pillar and waited for Sorrentino to appear.

After a while, Dirk heard a car engine approaching. A yellow VW van drove up the ramp and did a circuit of the level before stopping in front of the lift doors.

Out of the van stepped a man with a goatee beard and a woman with short, spiky red hair.

"Hey, Precious, I should sweep the area for feline activity," said the man.

"Drop it with the cat paranoia, Frank," replied the woman before shouting, "Hey, Sorrentino? You here?"

A bright flashlight beamed from a shadow beside the lift.

"What's with the interrogation lights, dude?" said Precious, shielding her eyes.

"That's far enough," said a female voice. "Let's see the money."

Frank pulled out an envelope and began to walk towards the voice.

"Throw it," said Sorrentino.

Frank lobbed the envelope into the shadow. After a moment's pause, a suitcase slid out into the light.

"This better be worth the money," said Precious.

"If you're not satisfied, you've got my number," replied Sorrentino.

"It was a pleasure doing business with you," said the man with the goatee beard, picking up the suitcase. Then he and the woman got back into their van and drove away.

Dirk waited behind for Sorrentino to show herself. When the flashlight went off Dirk saw a movement in the shadow by the lift. Then Sorrentino stepped into the light, revealing her face. She had a long nose, yellow eyes and grey skin covered in thin white spikes.

"You're a dragon," muttered Dirk.

Sorrentino spun round. "Who are you?" she demanded.

"The name's Dirk Dilly," he replied. "And I didn't catch your first name."

"My name's Mo. Mo Sorrentino. What's it to you, Mountain Dragon?"

"Mo? You're the dragon Kitelsky and Putz mentioned," said Dirk, approaching on all fours, his head lowered.

"How do you know Kitelsky and Putz?" snarled Sorrentino.

"Don't you ever worry about all those human lives you ruin?" said Dirk.

"Listen, I make some people happy, I make some people sad. What business is it of yours, anyway?" Sorrentino said, flicking out her claws threateningly.

"None at all," said Dirk, "but films of dragons make it my business."

"Ah, so that's what this is about," said Sorrentino.

"What's your involvement, Sorrentino?" Thick clouds of smoke gushed from Dirk's nose.

"Your fire don't scare me, Mountain Dragon," said Sorrentino, moving so she was within spitting distance of Dirk's face. He could hear a bubbling noise coming from her throat.

"I know what you're thinking," said Sorrentino. "Is she loaded with her day's poison? And to tell you the truth, I've kind of forgotten myself, but being as Desert Dragon poison is the deadliest in the world, you've got to ask yourself a question. *Do I feel lucky?* Well, do you? Do you, Dirk?"

"You watch too many movies, Mo," replied Dirk. "If you killed me here, you'd have to dispose of my body and I'm guessing you could do without that kind of hassle. Where's the footage?"

"Ah, who cares? I got paid already," replied the Desert Dragon. "I sold it, so what?"

"Sold it? What do you think you're playing at, Sorrentino? Do you want to start a war?"

"A war?" sneered Sorrentino. "Humans have caught weirder things on camera." She laughed. "This isn't the Middle Ages. People don't believe in us any more. One little film ain't gonna change that."

"Who did you sell it to?" said Dirk

"You just watched them drive away. They paid well too, more than I was expecting to get. Go ahead and get it back if you want, but I'd hurry, if I were you."

Dirk snarled. He ran to the edge of the car park and

looked down. The yellow van was waiting at the lights.

"This isn't the last you've seen of me," he said to Sorrentino.

"Do me a favour, call my receptionist and make an appointment next time," replied the Desert Dragon.

Dirk sent an angry burst of fire at Sorrentino and flew down to a nearby building.

Jumping over roofs, he followed the van across town. It was making slow progress with the early evening traffic, but after a while, the van turned off the main road. A couple more turns and it headed up a winding private road with a sign that said *Sands Hall* and a logo that Dirk recognized at once as belonging to Brant Buchanan's company, Global Sands.

"Super-rich rats," Dirk swore.

A row of security cameras lined the top of the gate. Dirk could go no further.

15

Had Dirk been able to follow the van into the grounds of Sands Hall he would have seen Brant Buchanan lead Precious and Frank into a cylindrical building surrounded by scaffolding.

"Nice library, man," said Frank. "You having work done?"

"I'm having some extra security measures put in," replied Buchanan, striding across the room and reaching for a book on a high shelf with a red spine and a tiny speck of white across the bottom.

"Hey, I recognize that," said Precious. "That's *Dragonlore* by Ivor Klingerflim."

"Indeed," said Brant Buchanan, tilting the book.

A section of book spines slid to the side and

revealed a TV screen set into the wall.

"That's some proper secret spy stuff, right there," said Frank.

"Yes," said Buchanan. "Now let's see what we have, shall we?"

He inserted a tape into a slot beside the screen and, after a moment, a desert appeared on TV. The sound of whistling wind filled the room. The shot panned across a desolate landscape dotted with strange trees with thick, twisted branches. *"That's nice. Hold that,"* said a voice on the tape and the camera stopped moving. *"Go in a little."* The camera zoomed in. Something moved in the shot. It was as though two of the strange trees were shifting in the distance. *"What's that?"* The camera zoomed in again. The picture fell out of focus for a moment and then refocused on the hazy horizon where two cactus-like creatures were fighting.

"What do you think?" asked Precious excitedly.

"Yeah, what do you think, man?" said Frank enthusiastically.

Brant Buchanan chose his words carefully. "It's a bit blurry, isn't it?" he said.

"Blurry?" exclaimed Frank, leaping in front of the screen. "We bring you never-seen-before footage of two Desert Dragons filmed yesterday and you call it blurry?"

"Calm down, dude," said Precious, anxious not to upset the billionaire.

"I am calm." Frank sounded anything but. "I just think he should appreciate what we've got here. This is solid-gold proof, man."

Buchanan laughed. "My friends," he said, "I thought I made it perfectly clear when I employed you that I have no doubt of the existence of dragons. None whatsoever. Please don't get me wrong. This footage will serve its purpose."

"What purpose?" asked Frank.

"Bait," replied Buchanan.

"What's that supposed to mean?" asked Precious.

Buchanan grinned and pulled out a remote control from his pocket. "It means I do not require further proof of the existence of dragons." He pressed a button and the desert was replaced by a map of the world. "From Ivor Klingerflim's book we know that there are dragons in every corner of the earth.

Varieties of the Desert Dragons you showed me exist not only in California, but in the Sahara, the Arabian, the Gobi... In fact, they reside in every great desert of the world."

As he spoke the map lit up the world's deserts.

"There are Mountain Dragons wherever there are mountains."

This time mountain ranges around the world lit up.

"The oceans are full of Sea Dragons and other even more fantastic beasts. The forests and jungles are alive with as many varieties of Tree Dragon as there are varieties of trees. The Arctic and Antarctic are rich with Snow Dragons. The sky itself is littered with sublimated Sky Dragons hiding among the clouds."

By the time he had finished speaking the entire map was lit up. It was so bright that Precious and Frank sheltered their eyes.

The screen went blank.

"There are even a few urban-based dragons," said Buchanan.

On the screen, a dragon crept around an office.

"Whoa, man," said Frank.

"You got an extreme close-up," said Precious, running her fingers through her red hair.

"But if you got stuff this good, why do you need us?" said Frank.

"I have employed you because knowing about dragons isn't enough for me. I intend to ensnare one," replied the billionaire.

As a thank you for the long day of filming, World Studios had given all the extras from the school concert scene free VIP passes to the movie theme park next door. So the next day, Mr and Mrs Bigsby had dropped Holly and Archie at the gates and gone shopping.

"We'll pick you up at three," said Mr Bigsby.

"Don't forget we have dinner at Brant Buchanan's mansion this evening," added Mrs Bigsby.

Holly was still wondering what this urgent work was that her stepmum had been brought over to do, but Mrs Bigsby was having too much of a good time to worry about it.

Holly was having a good time too. The theme park

was brilliant. All of the rides were based on films. There was loads to do and it was all free. Even better, the VIP tickets meant that wherever there was a long queue, Holly and Archie could jump it, and whenever they fancied a snack they didn't have to pay.

"This is the best holiday ever," Holly said as they entered an open-air walk-through jungle full of moving models of dinosaurs called Dinoworld.

"I'm here in the jungle with the lesser-spotted Holly Bigsby," said Archie, using the ice cream he was eating as a microphone. "Holly, tell me, what is it like being a VIP?"

"I think it's very V to be a VIP," said Holly.

"So you're saying that it's V V to be a VIP?"

"If not V V V," replied Holly, laughing so much she almost dropped her ice cream.

"This model represents a dimetrodon," said a young boy with an annoyingly loud voice, pointing at a plastic lizard beneath a plant. The lizard scuttled unconvincingly across the rock. "Interestingly, although it looks like a dinosaur it is actually an ancestor of mammals," continued the boy with a self-satisfied smile.

Holly and Archie moved quickly to the next section, but the boy followed them. "We're now entering the Triassic period, in which dinosaurs first appeared," he said.

A long-necked dinosaur loomed over them, its neck moving mechanically and a strange roaring sound coming from a speaker by its side.

"This is a plateosaurus." The boy was beginning to get on Holly's nerves. "And over here is the Pterosaur, a flying reptile. And here is a ... oh, that's not right. This isn't a dinosaur."

Holly and Archie looked at the model the boy was pointing at.

"Dinosaurs didn't have smoke coming out of their noses and they certainly weren't red and green."

Holly gasped and Archie almost dropped his ice cream. Standing frozen to the spot, moving his head robotically, was Dirk.

"How do you know what colour they were?" said Archie. "They could have been bright pink for all anyone knows. All they've ever found is fossils of bones."

"Well, that's not a dinosaur. It's a dragon and that's

stupid because dragons don't exist," said the boy, stamping his feet.

Dirk paused, then moved to look at the boy. "No one likes a know-it-all. Beat it, kid," he said.

"Th-th-that's so rude," stammered the boy, bursting into tears and running away.

"Dirk!" Holly threw her arms around his neck.

"And you're right, Archie, some of them *were* pink," said Dirk.

"You remember dinosaurs?" said Archie.

"I'm not that old," replied Dirk, "but I once met a dragon that claimed to have kept a pink tyrannosaurus rex as a pet. It was very loyal apparently but it did bite. Oh and it shed feathers everywhere."

"Dinosaurs never have feathers in films," said Archie.

"It just goes to show you can't believe everything you see in the movies," replied Dirk.

"What are you doing here?" asked Holly.

"Buchanan's got the film," said Dirk.

"Buchanan?" said Holly.

A group of Japanese tourists entered. Dirk froze and went back to his small robotic head movements.

"Oooo," they said, seeing him.

"Will you take a photo of us?" asked one of the tourists, handing a camera to Holly.

"Sure," she said.

They gathered around Dirk. Holly pretended to take the photo, but instead of pressing the shutter button, she pressed the off button. "That's a good one," she said, handing the camera back to the grateful tourists, who thanked her and moved on.

"So Buchanan is involved," said Holly.

"Seems so. Sorrentino sold him the film," said Dirk.

"Who's Sorrentino?" asked Holly.

"She's a dragon who hires herself out to humans to solve their problems."

"It sounds like what you do," said Holly.

"Yeah, except she doesn't mind people getting hurt... Oh, and she's got a receptionist."

"You've got Mrs Klingerflim," said Holly.

Dirk laughed, then froze again as a mother and her two children walked past. Once they had gone, Holly continued.

"You think Buchanan knows about you and me?" said Holly. "I mean, my stepmum hasn't exactly been busy since she's been here. If Buchanan suspects I know a dragon, he could be using me to get to you."

"We'll need to be extremely careful," said Dirk, "but I do need to get that film back and the place is covered in cameras."

"We're going round tonight for dinner," said Holly. "We could find out where he's keeping it."

"Good," said Dirk, "but be cautious. No blending. We can't take any risks if there's the slightest possibility that Buchanan suspects that you have a connection to me."

"OK," said Holly.

"And if I'm going to find a way in I could do with some details about the mansion," said Dirk.

"No problem," said Holly.

"Great, I'll come and see you later tonight at your house," said Dirk. "In the meantime I'm going to keep an eye on the two guys he's got working for him. Now, I better get out of here. I'll see you tonight."

Holly squeezed his right paw. "Bye, Dirk," she said.

"Hey, little lady, no touching the exhibits," said an official in a T-shirt with *Dinoworld* written on the front. "Some of them might bite," he added, with a false laugh. "No, but seriously, you really shouldn't touch them... Hey, I don't remember this fella." He looked at Dirk. "He's more like a dragon than a dinosaur, isn't he?" He reached up and pinched the skin on Dirk's cheek. "How do they make them so realistic?"

A low growl came from Dirk's throat.

"I thought you said no touching," said Holly.

"You're quite right, little lady," said the man, moving his hand away.

"Can you show us the way out?" asked Archie. "We're lost."

"Sure, follow me. It's right out of Triassic, past Jurassic and you're into the canteen where you can feast on one of our terrific dinoburgers. Don't worry, they're not made from real dinosaur." He sounded like he was reading from a script.

Dirk waited until they were out of sight before jumping up on to the roof of the Haunted House.

"Look, Mum, a dragon," said a little girl, holding a lollipop.

"Yes, lovely, dear, you've seen all sorts of things today, haven't you?" replied her mother.

PROD

17

DIR
CAM

During dinner at Brant Buchanan's that evening, Holly tried so hard to be on her best behaviour. She managed to be polite as they arrived at the mansion and as they took their places around the impressive table in the centre of the huge dining hall.

Not that the billionaire seemed especially interested in the children. For most of the meal, the adults talked about inflation and real estate and emerging markets and all the other boring things that adults talk about. Holly and Archie chatted among themselves. After dessert, Buchanan suggested that the grown-ups retire to the lounge for coffee while the children were welcome to take a look around.

"I'm afraid that having no children myself, there

are no toys or computer games in Sands Hall," he said, "but I'm sure you can find some way to amuse yourselves."

As they left the room and headed up the stairs Archie said, "That was easy."

It was a huge mansion. They took one room each, trying to make it look like they were playing a game of hide-and-seek, searching for places to hide. The rooms were stylishly but sparsely decorated, which made them quick to check, and it wasn't long before they were heading back downstairs. But the search downstairs proved equally fruitless.

"The thing is, we're looking for the stolen film," said Archie, "but surely he'll have converted it and uploaded it by now."

"Maybe," said Holly, "but remember what Tara said about how hard it is to get converted? There's a good chance it's still just the film. If we can find it, that is."

"What about in there?" asked Archie.

Across the floodlit courtyard was a cylindrical building surrounded by scaffolding. It had no windows and a curved transparent roof.

"Definitely worth checking," said Holly.

They snuck out and trotted down a set of concrete steps. At the bottom, they pushed the tarpaulin back and found that the door was unlocked. Holly stepped inside and looked up at the night sky through the glass ceiling.

"It's an observatory," said Holly.

Archie flicked a light switch, illuminating the bookshelves that lined the walls.

"It's a library," replied Archie.

"Have you noticed something odd?" Holly asked, looking up.

"What?"

"There are no cameras in here."

She was right. Unlike all the other rooms in Sands Hall there wasn't a single security camera.

"Why wouldn't there be cameras here?"

"Because he's got something to hide," replied Holly. "Look for a clue."

There were books on subjects from fly-fishing to fencing, histories of every country in the world, biographies of great leaders, explanations of astrology, astronomy and mythology. Then something caught Holly's eye. It was a red book spine with a small triangle of white at the bottom. It was sticking out slightly on a high shelf just out of reach.

"*Dragonlore*," she gasped, trying to jump up and reach the book. "It's too high."

"Try this." Archie pulled out four larger books from a lower shelf and placed them on top of each other.

Holly stood on top of the books and grabbed the spine of *Dragonlore*. She tried to pull it out but only succeeding in tilting it.

"It's not a book… It's a switch!" said Archie.

A section of books slid to the side revealing a blank screen. The screen flickered and then a desert landscape appeared.

"It's the film," said Holly.

They watched as the camera moved across the scene. They heard Tara's voice giving instructions to the cameraman. The shot zoomed in and found the two spiky dragons moving on the shimmering horizon, sending clouds of dust up as they fought.

"That's so cool," said Archie.

"But where's the actual film?" said Holly.

A voice outside interrupted them. "Holly, Archie,

come along now. It's time to go home." It was Mrs Bigsby.

"Come on, we'd better put everything back," said Archie.

"But we haven't found the film," protested Holly.

"At least we know it's in here somewhere," said Archie.

Holly pushed the book-lever back into position while Archie replaced the others on the shelf. The desert scene disappeared and the panel with the false book spines slid back into place.

Holly and Archie went back into the main building, where the others were standing in the hall.

"I trust that you found a way to amuse yourselves in my stuffy old house," said Mr Buchanan.

"We played hide-and-seek," said Holly.

"It was fun," added Archie.

"I'm glad it wasn't too boring for you," replied the billionaire.

PROD

18

DIR
CAM

Dirk had been unable to follow the yellow van into Brant Buchanan's mansion, but, before going to find Holly, he had waited for the van to leave and followed it back to a laundrette on the west side of town.

Now, he was following the van across town, enjoying himself as he leaped from roof to roof. He recited the opening lines from the voice-over that ran through *The Big Zero*.

"In some stories," Dirk muttered, "the kind they like to tell you in Hollywood, the good guys always win and the bad guys always lose. Well, I live in the real Hollywood and I can tell you that in real life it ain't like that. In my experience, the bad guys get their fair share of winning too."

Once the van had parked, its occupants climbed out.

"All I'm saying is that we got to give Buchanan something really good, Frank, dude," said Precious.

"That's what I'm talking about," replied Frank, slamming the car door shut. "It was a classic cover-up story – no pictures, no one remembers what happened. He's the most reliable source we got."

"Reliable? I think we must have different dictionaries."

"You know what I mean, Precious."

They walked to the end of the road where there was a bookshop called Unknown Worlds. Outside, a man in a mushroom hat strummed a guitar underneath some wind chimes. As Precious and Frank entered the shop Dirk caught a whiff of burning incense. Dirk knew the sort of place. Inside would be material on every conspiracy theory known to man. There would be books on angels, fairies, aliens and dragons, and not one word of truth in any of them.

When they came out, Frank was carrying a large pile of books.

"I don't know why you waste your time on this, man," said Precious. "When it comes to dragons, there's only one book you need." She pulled out a battered copy of *Dragonlore* and waved it in Frank's face.

"Yeah but *Dragonlore* ain't gonna help find –" Frank lowered his voice – "the Turning Stone. Imagine the sort of money Buchanan would pay for that. We could set up the business properly, rather than the back room of a laundrette."

"We've got to give him something solid," said Precious.

Frank stopped. "In *Dragonlore*, it says how some think Minertia had it. I think she buried it with the rest of her treasure."

"Hidden treasure… Dude, I worry about you sometimes. How are we ever going to get taken seriously with you going on about hidden treasure and alien cats?"

"I believe what I believe, Precious. Find Minertia's treasure, we find the Turning Stone."

Precious picked up the top book off the pile that Frank was carrying. "And you're going to find it in *Men are from Mars, Dragons are from Pluto*?"

"My mind is open, that's all I'm saying," replied Frank.

They reached the car and Precious opened the door so Frank could climb in with his books.

Dirk's mind was racing. He knew the Turning Stone was real. It was said that whoever possessed it would have power over all dragonkind. So was Frank's theory so ridiculous? It made sense that Minertia would have had it. That would explain why Vainclaw and Karnataka were desperate to get their hands on Minertia's treasure.

"Hey, Precious, that cat's looking at me."

A tabby cat was scratching itself against a nearby wall.

"It's got alien eyes, Precious," said Frank, slamming the door shut.

"You know, you got to get past the cat thing," said Precious, getting into the driver's seat. "It's holding you back, dude."

When Holly and Archie returned to the house, they ran upstairs to Holly's room, shut the door and went out on to the balcony.

"Dirk?" said Holly.

"I'm blended on the roof above you," said Dirk. "We need to be quick. I don't want to take any unnecessary risks. What news?"

"It's in the circular building surrounded by scaffolding. It's a library," said Holly. "There are cameras all around but none inside. We think Buchanan doesn't want anyone seeing what happens in there."

"Any indication that he suspects you?" asked Dirk.

"No, he let us run around wherever we wanted," said Holly. "If he knew about you and me, he'd be more cautious, wouldn't he?"

"Unless he *wanted* you to find the film," said Dirk.

"But it was you who discovered he had the film, not us," said Archie.

"True, but still be careful, both of you," said Dirk. "We shouldn't meet again. It's too risky."

"Will you go and get it tonight?" said Holly.

"No. I'll need to figure out a way around the cameras," said Dirk. "Besides, something else has come up. I'm going to be out of town for a short while."

"Isn't that a bit of a gamble?" said Archie.

"Maybe, but my gut tells me that anyone as wealthy as Buchanan is going to want to keep a secret like this to himself for a while."

"Where are you going?" asked Archie.

"I'm going underground," said Dirk.

PROD

19

DIR
CAM

Just outside the city, in a quiet spot, Dirk came to a standstill on a suitable rock and politely asked it to take him down. The rock, being rock, obliged unquestioningly.

He travelled for several hours in darkness and then the orange glow of earthlight filled the sphere of shifting stone. Past the lithosphere tunnel it grew lighter and the heat became uncomfortable.

Eventually, Dirk felt the rock beneath him pull away. He braced himself, remembering how hot the banks of the Outer Core had been the last time he visited. As he felt himself tumble down, he curled up into a ball, protecting his soft underbelly from the scorching pebbles by the fiery lake that hissed and bubbled angrily. He sprang to his feet and headed along the beach.

The Outer Core wasn't exactly a popular tourist retreat but eventually he found a wingless Firedrake sitting on the shore, using a long-handled ladle to fill a line of flasks with the contents of the lake. The Firedrake had tough skin, with rows of tiny holes on its back. A pair of crudely fashioned sunglasses, made from the same black metal as the ladle and flasks, rested on his upturned nose.

"Shute Hobcraft," said Dirk.

"Dirk Dilly, my main dragon," replied the Firedrake, looking up. "Watch this."

Shute picked up one of the flasks, opened it and poured its scolding contents into his mouth. He crouched down, with a look of concentration on his face, and suddenly a jet of steam shot from a hole on the lower part of his back with such force that it propelled him forwards. Dirk dodged out of the way as the Firedrake whizzed past him, spinning over and landing upside down on the beach in fits of giggles.

"What a rush, dude. Help me up, will you?"

Dirk pulled Shute to his feet.

"Still taking your job seriously, I see," said Dirk.

"Hey, I can't help it if I make work fun," said Shute.

Shute Hobcraft's job was to check how hot the Outer Core was. The slightest drop in temperature meant that a banished dragon was trying to escape from the Inner Core. If this happened Shute would alert the authorities who would catch the escapee.

"I've come to ask you about Minertia," said Dirk.

"Oh yeah, dude, she was one big dragon."

"You were the last one to see her before she was sent down. Any idea what she did with her treasure?" asked Dirk.

"You're not the first to ask me," said Shute. "Every so often, some gold-greedy dragon comes asking about it. The last time it was a Mountain Dragon, like yourself, and a Sea Dragon. I forget their names."

"Jegsy and Flotsam?" asked Dirk.

"That was them," said Shute. "They seemed like bad sorts to me. I didn't think looting was your bag, Dirk."

"It's not. I don't care about the gold," said Dirk.

"Well, I can't help. I've no idea what Minertia did with it." Shute downed the contents of the flask.

Steam shot from all of the holes on his back. "Woo hoo, that's hot!"

"Did she say anything to you at all?"

"She was more of a thinker than a speaker. She could read your mind, you know," said Shute. "I was wondering why she didn't try to make a run for it, because she only had three Drakes holding her down and like I say, she was a fair-sized dragon. She turned to me and I heard her speak in my head. She said, 'I helped define these laws. I will not break them.' Then she jumped straight in, not a second thought. It was pretty mad to watch."

"That's all she said?" said Dirk.

"Sorry, dude."

"Rats," said Dirk, wondering what to do next.

"You could go and ask her, I guess," said Shute.

"What do you mean?" asked Dirk.

"I mean, if I really wanted to know something like that I'd swim down to the Inner Core and ask her. She wouldn't tell you if you were a gold digger but she might if you had good intentions … providing she's still alive."

"Swim down through that?" Dirk stepped back

from the lake. "I'd die."

"Die, dude?" said Shute. "No way, this is the life force. Sure, it's hot. I'm not saying it won't sting a little but it won't kill you – it's where we all start life, isn't it?" Shute threw an empty flask into the lake. As it hit the surface, red boiling liquid splashed back and the flask sunk beneath the surface, sending black smoke up.

Dirk walked to the edge of the lake and looked in. He tried to think of an option that didn't involve having to swim through it. He could simply walk away and hope that Vainclaw had no better luck finding the Turning Stone. But Vainclaw wouldn't give up so easily and if he found it, then what? Ultimate war. And if Shute was right that Minertia could read minds then she would know Dirk didn't want it for himself. He looked at the scorching lake, grim determination in his eyes.

"You're going to do it, aren't you? That's what I like about you, dude. You're a thrill-seeker like me," said Shute gleefully. "Don't worry, I won't call the Dragnet on you. I'll allow for two heat dips, one when you go down, another when you come back up."

Dirk dipped a claw into the lava. It wasn't too bad. He tried a paw.

"Grearrghouch!" he screeched. "Rats in grass skirts, that's hot!"

"The trick is to just jump straight in," said Shute.

"See you around, Shute," said Dirk, gritting his teeth and wading into the lake.

The scorching liquid surrounded him, scalding the skin on his legs. Dirk took a deep breath and dived in, fully submerging his body. The agony was unspeakable. He would have screamed but to open his mouth would only have increased the pain. He felt his soft underbelly blister and harden. He swam down, feeling like he was being deep-fried. *Crispy-fried dragon*, he thought.

It was too much. He turned round and tried to swim back but he felt disorientated. He no longer knew which way was up. The more he swam the hotter he got. Even through his eyelids, the light was as intense as the heat. It was like swimming through the sun. *I'm going to die*, he thought. *Shute was wrong. This is going to kill me.*

His limbs gave up. He stopped moving. He was

too tired. He had no energy. *So this is how it ends,* he thought. *My life ends where it began, in the fire of the Outer Core.* Dirk felt strangely calmed by this idea.

Then a voice that was not his own appeared inside of his head, saying, *It is not your time to die just yet.* Something grabbed him. He was too weak to fight as it hauled him out of the liquid fire. Finally, he gasped for breath but his lungs were only filled with stale, hot, dry air.

Dirk Dilly, Dragon Detective, said the voice inside his head. *There are very few dragons who would come here without first being banished.*

Dirk prized his eyes open and squinted. Two burning circles, like a pair of suns scorched his eyeballs. The light that surrounded him was intense. The heat and humidity were relentless. He raised a claw to shield his eyes. The circles vanished and reappeared in what Dirk realized was a blink.

Two huge eyes and a dragon's face the size of a cliff loomed over him. The dragon herself was as big as a mountain. There was no need to ask her name. He recognized the voice. It hadn't changed in the thousand years since the last time he had heard it at the conference in the Himalayas.

"Minertia," he said, instinctively bowing.

It has been an age since I heard my name spoken. I already know why you're here, Dirk Dilly.

"How?" asked Dirk.

There are many angles on the surface of the earth – and many truths. Here, at the planet's centre, things are much clearer.

"Maybe to you," said Dirk, who had no clue what that meant.

You are here in search of the Turning Stone.

Minertia's cavernous mouth remained closed. Instead, her words appeared in Dirk's head.

"I want to hide it. Others are looking for it," said Dirk.

I know, said the ancient dragon. *I have seen all that has happened and I know all that will happen next.*

"You can predict the future?" said Dirk.

I can see how things will be, yes. You are trying to find the Turning Stone to prevent it falling into the claws of the one they call Vainclaw Grandin.

"Yes."

His are not the only claws that seek to grasp it, are they?

The words drifted through Dirk's clouded mind.

"No," he replied, thinking of his old friend Karnataka.

None shall acquire it, said Minertia.

"How can you be so sure?" asked Dirk.

Minertia's enormous mouth curled up at the edge. She was smiling. *Rest assured, the stone will not be found. Whoever succeeds in this tussle, they will have to persuade their fellow dragons that theirs is the cause worth dying for without the stone.*

"But if you know what happens then…"

Dirk hesitated so Minertia finished the sentence for him. *I should keep that to myself. You are quite right.*

"You could come back with me," said Dirk.

I could but I will not, she replied. *I was banished and I am no less guilty now than I was then. I breached the forbidden divide.*

"You mean that you did attack humans?" said Dirk.

No. In the council's eyes it was much worse than that. I tried to make peace with the humans.

"Peace?"

Yes. The Kinghorns are right about one thing. We can hide no longer. It is time to come out into the open before we are discovered. I believed we should emerge, not in war as they would have it, but in peace. We once worked side by side. We could do so again.

"If you believe that, why do you remain here in hiding?"

I am not in hiding. My banishment was an inevitable event in a sequence of events that result in you, Dirk Dilly, forging a new future alongside humanity.

"Me?" said Dirk.

The smiled widened. Yes, but fear not, you have many adventures ahead of you before you need to worry about that. Keep your secrets for now. You will know when the time has come, the time to step out into the light. Now, you must go, back through the liquid fire, across the shore and up to the surface. You have work to do, Mr Dilly.

"You mean I need to recover the film?" he said.

Yes, but more than that. You need to find Skull Rock.

21

Holly and Archie were having a great holiday. They had walked down the star-paved streets full of people dressed up as famous movie characters, visited movie sets and been to the beach. Even getting to see Dirk and help him find the missing film felt like a treat, although Holly was beginning to wonder when she was next going to hear from him.

Mrs Bigsby had attended a couple of meetings but she seemed more relaxed than ever. Archie never brought up his family and Holly didn't ask. It was as though they had all left their cares behind them in London.

They were arriving back at their house from an afternoon at the cinema when they found Miss

Gilfeather walking briskly up their drive.

"I'm sorry to bother you, Mr and Mrs Bigsby," she said.

"Not at all," said Holly's dad. "Miss … er…"

"Gilfeather," said Holly.

"Please, call me Vivian," she said. "I wonder whether I could borrow Holly and Archie for a short while."

Mr Bigsby said that would be fine. As Miss Gilfeather led them back down the drive, through the gates and next door to Petal's house, Holly asked, "What do you need us for?"

Miss Gilfeather stopped and spoke very quietly. "It's Petal. She's terribly upset. Do you know, I actually feel sorry for her. Nothing I say helps, her mother is incommunicado and none of her other friends are answering the phone. So I thought maybe you could talk to her."

"But she hates us," said Holly.

Miss Gilfeather looked at Holly, then at Archie and smiled. "Oh, I don't think so. In fact, in her own little obnoxious way, I think she's rather fond of you. But that isn't the point. The point is she's upset and

I'm asking you to make her feel better."

She took them inside and showed them into the lounge, where Petal was sitting on a sofa in the shape of a pair of lips. Her face was blotchy and red from crying. In front of her was a TV, paused on a smiley-faced presenter with the words *Hollywood Gossip* behind her.

Holly and Archie looked at each other, then back at Petal.

"Hi, Petal," said Archie.

"Leave me alone. This is a disaster," she replied, waving a hand dismissively. "It's not fair. It's not even true. They shouldn't be allowed to tell lies like that. Chase is coming over in a minute. He'll put things right."

"Put what right? What's wrong?" asked Holly.

She pressed the play button on the remote control.

"… And now the latest gossip from tinsel town," said the presenter. "Rumour has it that *Petal: The Movie*, the film version of Petal Moses' autobiography, is set to be a total flop." Behind her an unflattering photo of Petal appeared. She was mid-blink and chewing gum. Seeing it, Petal howled in misery.

"Our spies on set say that Miss Moses is following in her mother's footsteps." The presenter paused, then added, "She's an awful actress too. Hollywood legend, Chase Lampton, must be worried about the impact the film will have on his flagging career, not to mention that of his son, Dante. Mr Lampton refused to speak to our reporter." The picture of Petal was replaced by images of Chase quickly getting into the back of a car, then being driven away.

"His silence speaks volumes," continued the presenter. "And, in spite of her executive producer status, Petal's oh-so-famous mother has been strangely distant from the project. Suspiciously, as her daughter's movie looks to become the biggest turkey this side of Christmas, her mum is off recording a new album. A case of *Don't blame me*, perhaps."

Petal hit the pause button and the picture froze on the presenter's plastic smile again.

"Wow…" said Archie.

Holly tried to think of something better to say. She wasn't exactly a fan of Petal but, seeing her so upset, she felt sorry for her.

"It's simply terrible," said Petal.

"But these are just rumours," said Holly. "No one's even seen the film yet."

"That's very true," said Chase Lampton, staggering into the room, closely followed by Miss Gilfeather.

"Mr Lampton, I must insist you leave," she said.

"Now, Vivian," he replied, "I do wish you'd chase me call… No, that's not right. Call me Chase. That's it!"

"I'll do no such thing. Have you been drinking?"

"Just a couple," replied Chase, lurching to the side but steadying himself on a silver statue of a prancing unicorn.

"Now come along, you are in no fit state."

"I'll tell you what's in no fit state," said Chase, flopping on to the sofa next to Petal. "*Petal: The Movie*. It's a piece of junk. One more flop, the studio said. This was my last chance and what have I done? I've taken a kids' film and made a disaster movie…" Chase fell back, laughing at his joke. Petal burst into tears.

Holly and Archie glanced at each other.

"Mr Lampton!" Miss Gilfeather squawked. "Are you telling this twelve-year-old girl that the film she has spent all summer making is no good? Are you saying that after one bad report on some silly gossip show you're giving up on it? Is that what you're suggesting?"

Chase Lampton stopped laughing. He sat up straight. Her words seemed to have sobered him up. He looked at the floor and mumbled, "No, Miss Gilfeather."

"I'm sorry?" she said.

"It'll be fine." Chase turned to Petal who had stopped crying. "It's just Hollywood rumours, Petal. It's going to be a monumental movie."

"Really?" said Petal.

Chase stood up, avoiding eye contact with Petal. "Yeah, of course. We'll put a kicking soundtrack on it, lots of quick cuts. It'll be great. And hey, it's the wrap party tomorrow night. I'll get Tara to invite everyone who's anyone. Come the next morning, everyone will be saying what a fantastic movie it's going to be. Hollywood folk are as easily distracted as a cat with tinsel. Why do you think they call it tinsel town? You two should come," he said, pointing at Archie and Holly. "And, of course, you, Vivian. You'll save a dance for me, won't you?" He tried to demonstrate this with a fancy dance step but lost his footing, tripped on a leopard-skin rug and fell over with a **THUD**.

"I think we'd better take you home," said Miss Gilfeather, picking him up off the floor and dragging him to the door. "Come along."

"See you all at the party tomorrow night," said Chase.

"Blimey," said Archie once he was gone. "That was odd."

"You see," said Petal. "I knew Chase would make it all better. The film will be great. I'll have to buy a new dress for the party, of course."

"But—" Holly's protest was cut short by a nudge in the ribs from Archie.

"It's better than crying," he muttered through his teeth. "See you at the party, Petal," he said out loud.

"I can't really see why you're invited. You were only extras, after all," she replied.

Archie yanked Holly out of the room before she could respond. Outside, Miss Gilfeather had just managed to shove Chase into the back of his car.

"How is she?" asked Miss Gilfeather.

"Back to normal," replied Holly.

PROD

22

DIR
CAM

It was a long journey from the banks of the Outer Core to the surface and Dirk was pleased to finally cool down. He spent the duration of the journey thinking about what Minertia had said and finalising his plan for getting the film back.

The rock pulled away above his head to reveal the early morning sky. Dirk had no idea how long he had been gone. He was on a hill from which he could see the outskirts of Los Angeles. He headed down the hill and travelled across rooftops, then found a truck going in the right direction, jumped on top and blended with it.

Still avoiding Kitelsky and Putz, he steered clear of the Hollywood sign, instead heading to the laundrette with the yellow van parked outside. Dirk kept watch from the curved roof of a Chinese restaurant, camouflaging himself with the garish dragon statues until, eventually, the van's owners emerged.

"This is a proper game changer," enthused Frank.

"Maybe," said Precious. "It's still a long shot, dude."

"Yeah, but the Turning Stone," replied Frank. "We know where it is."

"You mean we know where it was last seen."

Frank produced a piece of paper. "It says it all in this article, 'The Summit of Skull Rock', and you've seen the name of the author, right? This is what Buchanan wants. Control the Turning Stone, control the dragons."

"Let's not get ahead of ourselves," said Precious. "But yes, we need to talk to Buchanan."

They got into the van and slammed the doors shut. Dirk was about to follow when he felt a sharp pain in his tail. He turned to see Kitelsky's claws digging into his skin. A bubbling noise came from his throat.

"So, you go sneaking off without us, disappear for days, then we find you here. This ain't no vacation, Dilly."

"Yeah, we got scores to settle." Putz stuck his head up from behind the long body of a dragon statue.

"You spike-headed idiots," hissed Dirk angrily. "I'm in the middle of the investigation."

"What you found out then?" asked Kitelsky.

"The film was stolen by Mo Sorrentino," Dirk replied.

"Mo?" said Putz.

"That's right. She runs a business in town, ruining people's lives. She was the one who sold the film."

"That no-good double-crosser!" said Kitelsky.

"So where's the film now?" asked Putz.

"It's with a human called Brant Buchanan but there are more important things to deal with first. Have you heard of Skull Rock?"

"Sure, it's back in the desert," said Kitelsky.

"I need you to take me there," said Dirk.

"We'll take you there as soon as we have the film," said Kitelsky.

"That's right," said Putz.

Dirk growled. The Turning Stone was important but so was the missing film. "OK, here's the deal," he said. "We'll go and get the film, then you take me to Skull Rock. OK?"

Kitelsky and Putz looked at each other and nodded.

"Let's go get it, Dilly," said Kitelsky.

23

"Oh yes, I've already had lots of other roles offered," Petal was saying to a circle of reporters. "Except they're all for parts playing, well, little girls. My agent thinks it very important that I don't get pigeon-holed at this stage in my career. That's the problem with Hollywood – everyone wants to put you in a box."

"I wish we could put her in a box," said Archie.

"And post it to the moon," added Holly.

The party to celebrate the end of filming was being held at World Studios on the set of Little Hope Village Hall. The wooden chairs had been cleared to one side and on the stage a jazz trio was playing far too quietly to be heard above the throng of people. Holly and Archie had spent a while trying to spot famous people, but the novelty soon wore off when most of them were "that bloke from that thing about the big missile" or "that woman who played an alien in that film about the world blowing up" or "the voice of that cartoon cat."

"I'm starving," said Archie. "We need to find some of those waiters with the food trays."

On their way across the room they saw Miss Gilfeather, talking to Chase Lampton. Her auburn hair was down around her shoulders and she was wearing a black silk dress.

"Hi, Miss Gilfeather, you look nice," said Holly.

"Thank you, Holly. I feel sorry for those poor musicians on stage. I can't hear a note they're playing with all these awful film people talking," she replied. She turned to Chase, who had slid his sunglasses into the pocket of his black suit jacket. "Now, Mr Lampton, I think you owe these two an apology."

The director looked at them. "I'm very sorry for my shameful appearance yesterday. I was tired and there was no excuse for my behaviour." He looked at Miss Gilfeather. "How was that?"

"It was a passable apology," replied Miss Gilfeather.

"Petal seems to be back on form," Holly observed.

"Shallow waters are easily calmed," said Miss Gilfeather. "Are you having a nice time?"

"Yes, thanks," said Archie and Holly. "We're off to find some food."

"If you see my son on your travels can you ask him to come find me? It's almost speech time." Chase held out his champagne glass for a top up from a waiter.

Holly and Archie continued through the crowd.

"There's Dante," said Archie.

Holly had spotted him too. He was in a corner talking excitedly to another boy. The boy raised a hand and smoothed down his hair, edging away from the director's son, nervously glancing around.

"It's Callum," said Holly, making her way over.

"Who?" said Archie.

"Callum Thackley, the person Dante was supposed to be playing."

"The Prime Minister's son?! I've got to meet him," said Archie, following her.

They reached the two boys and Callum's dark eyes flickered briefly to look at Holly. He edged away.

"Hey, guys," said Dante. "Look who it is. I've been

working on my accent, not that it matters now we've wrapped, but I reckon I came pretty close, eh, Callum old bean?"

Archie offered his hand but Callum let out a nervous giggle and shrank away. Dante laughed.

"I really wish we'd met before I did the film," he said, imitating Callum's movements.

"Dante, your dad's looking for you. He said something about a speech," said Holly.

"Right, I'll see you later, Callum." Dante slapped him on the shoulder.

Callum tensed up, smoothed down his hair, then looked away.

"I love this guy," said Dante, before leaving to find his dad.

"How are you, Callum?" said Holly.

He edged closer, still avoiding her gaze, and spoke quickly, breathlessly. "They say I'm making progress but only because I pretend that it's not true. I say I know the monsters are in my head because that's what they want to hear. I say I want to get better and I don't believe these things. But Callum lies. They are there, Holly knows. They are real, with real claws and real teeth and real flames and real anger. Soon everyone will know, won't they?"

Holly and Archie exchanged a glance.

"Has he been in contact again?"

Callum didn't respond.

"Vainclaw," said Holly. "Has he spoken to you recently?"

"He's always there, in my head, he's always with me, soon he'll come back for me and—"

Something behind Holly made him stop talking. Holly and Archie turned round to find Brant Buchanan standing behind them.

"Ah. I was hoping you'd get a chance to meet my house guest," he said.

"Callum's staying with you?" said Holly.

"His father is an old friend of mine," said Buchanan, "and Callum's been through so much, I thought he deserved a holiday. You used to go to school together, didn't you? What an appropriate setting for a reunion." He motioned to the film set. "I expect it brings back all sorts of memories."

"Excuse me… Hi, everyone," a voice was saying through the microphone. The crowd fell quiet. Tara

Leggett was standing on the stage, nervously tapping her glass. "Hi. Thanks. Ladies and gentlemen, I'm proud to give you Chase Lampton, his son, Dante Lampton, and the leading lady herself, Petal Moses."

The three of them walked on to the stage to the sound of applause. Petal was beaming with pride. Chase took the microphone. "Thanks, Tara." He addressed the crowd. "My old man used to say that making movies is like making a cake. All you need are the right ingredients, the right amount of time and a hungry audience. Well, for this particular cake we—"

The sound of a mobile phone ringing interrupted him.

"… I'm sorry, that's mine," said Chase, laughing. "I meant to turn it off. Just one second." He pulled the phone from his jacket and answered it. "Hi, I'm kind of busy right now," he said, winking at the crowd. The audience laughed too but Chase's face suddenly fell. "I see, right," he said seriously, stepping back from the microphone. For a moment no one was sure what to do. Petal and Dante stood grinning uncomfortably, glancing at Chase.

After a minute, the director returned to the

microphone. "Ladies and gentlemen, there is no cause for alarm but I need you all to leave the building as calmly as you can. There is no danger, but I've been informed that a fire has started in another part of the studio." A concerned hum rose up in the hall. Chase raised his voice over it and said, "As I say, nothing to worry about but studio regulations require that all hangers must be evacuated. I'm sorry for the inconvenience."

The crowd turned and made for the door. Buchanan placed a hand on Callum's shoulder and led him out.

"Why would Callum be staying with Buchanan?" said Holly as they shuffled out.

"It makes sense that he would know his dad. I mean, a man like Buchanan must know loads of important people," said Archie.

"I suppose," said Holly. "But Buchanan's interested in dragons and Callum's been in contact with the most dangerous dragon of all. It's not good."

Outside, the fire smelled like burning chemicals. Fire wardens in yellow bibs were showing everyone where to go. As they rounded a corner, they saw the blaze in a nearby building. Three fire engines had arrived and firefighters were trying to keep it under control, while others were making sure that no one got too near.

Holly and Archie found Chase and Dante standing in the front row watching the flames. Dante turned round and stared at them. He looked upset and his voice trembled as he spoke. "P-P-Petal's in there," he said.

"What?" said Holly.

"Petal's over there talking to that woman who played someone in that thing about a giant octopus," said Archie, indicating where Petal was standing chatting to a vaguely familiar actress.

"Not her," snapped Dante, "the film. The whole film. It was all in there. It's all gone."

"Gone?" said Holly and Archie together.

"That's right," said Chase. "They were digitizing the tapes when the place caught fire." Holly looked up at the director. Perhaps it was a trick of the light but she thought she saw the curve of a smile appear at the corners of his mouth. "You realize, Dante," he said, "that everything we worked for over these past few months has just gone up in smoke. Let's go get a bagel."

PROD

24

DIR
CAM

While the fire was raging in World Studios, on the other side of the city, three dragons were hiding in a row of leafy trees behind Sands Hall.

"What's this Blue-canon want with a film of us anyway?" said Kitelsky.

"Buchanan," corrected Dirk, "and I don't know."

"Who cares? If it's in there, I say we get it," said Putz.

Dirk blocked his way. "You'll do as I say unless you want your cameo turning into a leading role. The place is covered in security cameras."

"So how do we avoid being seen then?" asked Kitelsky.

"We cut the power," said Dirk.

Dirk pointed out a small red-brick structure to Kitelsky and Putz.

"That's the substation where the electricity comes into the building," said Dirk.

"So we just need to trash and smash it," said Putz, once again trying to edge forwards.

"Wait," said Dirk. "There are cameras pointing at that too."

"So what do you suggest?" said Kitelsky irritably.

"There's a vent on top, directly in the middle. I need one of you to spit poison through it. It should burn straight through the equipment and short the whole place. But you can't break your cover. You need to hit it from here."

"That's impossible," said Kitelsky.

"It's not impossible," said Putz. "We used to play target practice on that old rock up in Beggar's Canyon back home. That was about the same distance."

"If you think it's so easy, you do it," said Kitelsky.

"OK, I will," said Putz.

He looked at the target, took aim and titled his head back. A bubbling noise came from his throat. Dirk and Kitelsky watched anxiously. Suddenly Putz made a gagging sound and a stream of fluorescent green liquid shot from his throat, flying through the air, arcing, then heading down towards the substation.

But it overshot and hit a pot plant, melting straight through both the plant and the pot.

"Get out of the way. I'll do it," said Kitelsky. "I always was a better shot than you."

"Don't go any further than the edge of the trees," warned Dirk, as Kitelsky crept forwards and took aim. Kitelsky did the same as Putz, only this time the poison was right on target.

There was an electrical fizzing followed by a loud **CRACK** and every light in and around the mansion went out, including the little red lights on the security cameras.

"Good shot," said Dirk. "Now stay here."

"No way, we're comin' with you," said Kitelsky.

"Yeah, that's right, with you," said Putz.

"Listen, I haven't got time for this. There may still be humans in there and, if so, they're going to come running out, wondering what the problem is, and we don't want them to find that the problem is a bunch of dragons creeping around. Now, stay here," said Dirk.

He flew over the garden. His wings still ached from his recent swim through the Outer Core. He landed on top of the cylindrical building, careful to avoid the glass roof. He was relieved to see no one rushing out to find out what was going on. It looked like the place really was empty.

He licked his left paw and stuck it on to the glass, then extended a claw on his right and carefully cut a circular hole, which he lifted away and slid to one side. He dropped into the moonlit room. He quickly searched the room until he discovered the false wall of books. He prized it open to reveal the TV screen. With no electricity, it was blank. He reached up and felt around the side, trying to locate a wire.

"You found it yet?" said a voice above him.

Dirk glanced up and saw Kitelsky standing on the glass roof, his spiky head peeking through the hole.

"I told you to stay back," said Dirk.

"Relax, there ain't no one here," he said.

"Yeah, relax, we're being careful." Putz landed on the glass, which began to show signs of strain under the weight of the two dragons on it.

"Get off the glass, you idiots," said Dirk.

The glass creaked as a crack snaked across it like a slow-motion lightning bolt.

"Hey, that ain't very friendly," said Putz.

"It's not strong enough to support two—"

Dirk's words were cut short by the sound of shattering. He ducked and shielded his eyes from the shards of glass that rained down. Along with the glass came the two Desert Dragons, landing on top of him, their spikes jabbing painfully into his skin. The sound of tinkling glass lingered in the air for a few seconds, then the room fell silent.

"Get off me!" snarled Dirk, white smoke billowing from his nostrils.

Kitelsky and Putz climbed off and stood back. Dirk stood up and shook the bits of glass off his back.

"Watch it! You almost got me in the eye," said Kitelsky.

Dirk flew across the room, grabbing Kitelsky and slamming him into a wall of books that fell down, whacking them both on the head.

"Listen, you no-good desert rat," said Dirk. "It's your necks I'm trying to save here."

"What are all these things?" Putz picked up a fallen book.

"They're called books," said Dirk, releasing Kitelsky and snatching it off Putz. "But we're looking for a film."

He returned to the TV screen and groped around until he found a black wire running behind the shelves. He followed it down, knocking away the books as he did so, until he came to computer console. With his claw he pushed a button on the side. To his surprise, the button turned green and the screen flickered to life.

"Hey, that's us," said Kitelsky.

Dirk spun around. On the screen was the film of the two Desert Dragons.

"I never seen myself before. I got some good moves," said Putz.

"How can it be playing when we've cut the pow—" Dirk started. "Quick, get out!"

But as he spoke, sheets of solid metal shot up in front of the bookshelves and across the floor, knocking the dragons off their feet. The same happened over the top, blocking out the moonlight. It all happened too quickly for them to get out. Dirk flicked out his claws and rammed them into the wall of metal. But the hole he made quickly re-formed. He tried again but the same thing happened.

"What's going on?" said Kitelsky.

"Help me," said Dirk.

All three dragons went to work on the walls with teeth and claws, but each time they ripped a piece open it healed itself before they could make the hole any bigger. A voice behind them caused them to stop.

"Welcome," it said.

They looked up at the screen, where the voice had come from. The image of the desert had been replaced by a silver-haired man. Brant Buchanan smiled.

"I'm sorry that I'm not here to greet you personally," said the pre-recorded image, "but rest assured I will be with you very shortly. In the meantime, please enjoy this short feature."

"What's going on?" said Kitelsky.

Buchanan's image was replaced by footage of an office. Dirk recognized it at once as Buchanan's secret London lab. It cut to a different angle, then another, and then the screen split so he could see three alternative viewpoints.

"Hey, that looks like you, Dilly," said Putz.

Dirk watched with dismay as he saw himself drop into the office, look around, reach up and help Holly in.

"A human," said Kitelsky. "Why, you double-crossin' no-good dragon!"

"Looks like we're all movie stars now," said Putz.

When Petal learned about the film being destroyed, she let out a piercing scream, cried, "Someone's to blame!", then phoned her mum, who told her what to do.

"I have to take her for an emergency meeting with her lawyer," Miss Gilfeather told Holly and Archie, rolling her eyes. "Mr Buchanan has kindly offered to take you home."

Holly had been trying to steer clear of Buchanan so was pleased that he sat in the front seat beside his driver, leaving the backseat for her, Archie and Callum.

"You do have to feel sorry for Petal," said Holly. "All that work."

"I'm sure she'll get over it," said Archie.

"Her life story has been destroyed in a fire." Callum

smoothed down his hair. "Callum knows about burning. Callum knows about destruction."

"You're a lot of fun," said Archie. "Has anyone ever told you that?"

Callum giggled nervously.

Buchanan's phone rang. He answered it. "Ah, excellent timing," he said. "Meet me at Sands Hall. You can give me the information you're so excited about and I've got something to show you… Yes, see you shortly." He hung up and turned round to face Holly. "I'll take you home but first there's something I'd like to show you at the mansion."

"What is it?" asked Holly suspiciously.

Buchanan's grey eyes sparkled with excitement. "Have you ever played poker, Holly? No, of course not, you're too young," he said. "There's an expression in the game: to show one's hand. It means that all the players reveal what they're holding. No more bluffing, no more bets. It normally indicates the end of the game. Well, Holly Bigsby, our little game is also coming to an end. I think it's time to show our hands."

"What are you talking about?" she said, trying not to look at Archie.

"I mean no more secrets, Holly," said Buchanan.

"He knows, he knows about the monsters," said Callum. "He knows the truth."

"What are you talking about?" said Holly, trying to laugh it off.

"I said no more bluffing," snapped Buchanan, pressing a button, causing a screen to appear. "Now let me show you a little film that *I've* made. It's low budget and the camera work is a little shaky in places but it's got a terrific plot and I think you'll warm to the actors."

Holly gasped. On the screen, Dirk and she were breaking into Brant Buchanan's laboratory.

"The monster," said Callum, watching Dirk. He looked away, fidgeting nervously.

The shot cut to Holly and Archie standing in the library in Sands Hall.

"Why wouldn't there be cameras here?" asked Archie on the screen.

"Because he's got something to hide," replied Holly.

"Very astute," said Buchanan. "Except, of course there are cameras. Just extremely well-hidden ones. You see, unlike World Studios, I am more cautious with my films. Watch, this is my favourite scene now."

The shot changed again to show the exterior of the house where Holly and Archie had been staying. It was dark but the camera zoomed in to find Holly and Archie standing on a balcony talking to an almost – but not entirely – invisible dragon on the roof.

"I believe it's called blending, a skill unique to the Mountain Dragon," said Mr Buchanan.

They heard Dirk say, "My gut tells me that anyone as wealthy as Buchanan is going to want to keep a secret like this to himself for a while."

"He's quite right," said Mr Buchanan. "You see, I've been watching and listening to everything you've done and said since I called you here in the first place."

Holly felt dizzy. Her hands were shaking, but she felt Archie take one of them and grip it tightly.

"You'll never find him. No one will believe you," Archie said firmly. "People will say you faked this with special effects, that you're a mad rich man with too much time on your hands. You'll end up a gibbering wreck like Callum with monsters in your head."

"The monsters are crawling out of my head," said Callum.

"I have no interest in letting everyone in on our secret, Mr Snellgrove. Not yet," said Buchanan.

"Then what do you want?" said Holly.

"Want?" said Buchanan, as though seeing how the word tasted in his mouth. "For years I haven't *wanted* for anything. I did or I had. I never wanted. And then you appeared with your dragon friend and gave me something new to *want*." He leaned forwards. "I want a dragon. I want *your* dragon."

"You'll never catch him," said Holly.

"Ah, but thanks to you I already have," said Buchanan. "When I flew your family out here, I had no need for your mother, but I felt sure you were the key to acquiring a dragon. And I was right as usual. When you called Mr Dilly about the missing film, a plan formulated. I knew that the only way for him to retrieve it from the library would be to cut the electricity supply at the substation but he wasn't to know that I also have a back-up generator. Tonight, while we were at the party, the power went off and the generator kicked in. Do you know what that means? It means that, awaiting us in my library is a real, live fire-breathing dragon."

"He'll escape. Dragon claws can cut through anything," said Holly.

"As you proved when you cut through the hole in my laboratory roof," said Buchanan, pressing a button in the armrest and skipping back to the footage of Dirk and Holly in the laboratory. On the film, Holly had just run back into the room and she and Dirk were hiding.

Holly was relieved to see that she was not in shot when she blended with the sofa. At least that secret remained intact.

"The challenge was how to hold a creature that can tear through anything. Tricky. It was Weaver who came up with the answer. What's that stuff called again?"

"IMM, Intelligent Memory Metal," replied Weaver.

"Ah yes, that's it. Intelligent Memory Metal, amazing stuff. It's as strong as titanium and it instantly reforms when broken," said Buchanan. "It was produced for military use but no army has been able to afford it. I, on the other hand, had a little loose change, so I used it to create a dragon trap. I'll be intrigued to see how Mr Dilly is dealing with it."

Callum, whose eyes had been drawn to the screen, suddenly squealed and glanced at Holly. "I remember him. At Little Hope. He made my master go away."

"Vainclaw isn't your master," said Holly.

"Vainclaw Grandin," said Buchanan. "Yes, he sounds like a fascinating character."

Holly felt utterly defeated. Brant Buchanan knew everything and it was her fault. "Why?" she said quietly.

Buchanan turned back to face the road. "The secret to a successful business empire is to keep one step ahead of your competitors. If you know something they don't, you are stronger than they are. I'm already strong. I already know more than most. Imagine the strength this knowledge will give me."

Weaver took a right turn, taking them up the driveway that led to Sands Hall. They passed another car going down the hill, black with darkened windows.

"Who is that?" asked Buchanan.

"Probably just a lost tourist who saw the gates and turned round," said Weaver.

The gates buzzed open and Weaver parked the

car next to a yellow VW van. A man with a goatee beard and a woman with short red hair got out of the van as Buchanan, Callum, Holly and Archie stepped out of the car. The woman said, "Hey, Buchanan, how you doing?"

"Good evening, Precious. Hello, Frank," said Buchanan. "So, are you ready to see our catch of the day?"

"You bet, but what's with the kids? Looks like you're throwing a kids' party, man," said Frank.

"If I were, I'd know where to find the clowns," replied Buchanan. He turned to Holly. "Frank and Precious have been on a fact-finding mission for me. They suggested that Callum might be a useful houseguest. His father was more than happy to let him visit, wasn't he, Callum?"

"Dad is scared of Callum," said Callum. "He can't remember what happened at the concert but he remembers the fear. I see it in his eyes."

"Yeah, the concert," said Frank. "No footage, no one remembering anything, that concert was a classic cover-up, man."

"But forget that. Now we got something really

juicy, man," said Precious.

"All in good time," said Brant Buchanan, leading them through the garden, down the steps and round the corner to the library, surrounded by scaffolding. Weaver pulled away the tarpaulin and opened the door to reveal a sheet of metal behind it.

"You see," said Mr Buchanan, tapping the metal.

Callum was jabbering madly, "They're in there. They're in there. The monsters are in there."

"First contact with a real dragon, man," said Frank.

"Weaver, open it up," said Buchanan.

"Are you sure that's wise?" said Weaver.

Buchanan placed a hand firmly on Holly's shoulder. "Oh yes, I think we'll be OK, don't you, Holly?"

Weaver adjusted his wristwatch, then pressed a button on the side of the door and the metal sheet disappeared into the ground. He stood back.

The room was dark inside.

"You can come out now, Mr Dilly," called Buchanan.

They waited.

Nothing happened.

"Weaver," said Mr Buchanan.

Weaver nodded. With his right hand hovering

over his wristwatch, he stepped into the library. The light came on automatically.

"Well?" said the billionaire. "What have we got?"

"There's nothing here, sir," said Weaver, stepping out. "The top has been opened. The dragon's escaped."

Stuck inside the giant tin can, awaiting whatever fate lay outside, Dirk felt like a baked bean, which reminded him that, on top of being tricked, trapped and set up he was also starving.

"You've led us into a fine old mess, Dilly," said Kitelsky, pacing round the circular room.

"It ain't his fault," said Putz. "We followed him here."

"Either way, I'm itching to rumble and I got a hankerin' to rumble with Dirk Dilly, the dirty double-crossin' dragon detective," said Kitelsky, skulking towards Dirk.

Dirk spat a mouthful of fire at him, causing Kitelsky to yelp in pain. "It's a shame you've used up your poison then, isn't it?" snarled Dirk. "Back off, Kitelsky."

The three trapped dragons stared at each other.

"What is that?" said Dirk, noticing that the end

of Putz's nose was illuminated, as though a torch was shining on it from above.

"I don't know," said Putz, trying to look at it and going cross-eyed in the process.

Dirk looked up and saw that the metal ceiling was retracting, revealing the night sky above. Moonlight was, once more, spilling into the room.

"What's going on?" said Putz.

"Come on," said Dirk. "Follow me."

With a flap of his wings he reached the rim of the building, where he could see that the grounds were floodlit; the security cameras were back on. One swivelled on its stick to point at him. Dirk sent an angry burst of fire at it, causing it to instantly blow up, reducing it to a blackened crisp. Something caught his eye in the car park. A dark figure got into a black car with tinted windows. Dirk was unable to make out their features, but he spotted the wide-brimmed hat. The engine started and the car drove away.

Kitelsky and Putz joined him on top of the building.

"What happened?" asked Kitelsky.

"I don't know," said Dirk.

"What now?" said Putz.

The sound of another car engine was approaching.

"We get out of here. Buchanan will have to wait," said Dirk. "Take me to Skull Rock."

26

As the dragons left the library, there was no avoiding being caught on camera, but Dirk knew he would have to worry about that later. The Turning Stone was more important right now.

They headed across the rooftops, out of town.

"Which way is Skull Rock?" said Dirk, as they left the city lights behind them and entered the dark desert. Scraggy plant life caught on his claws and dragged along behind him. He shook his leg free and wished he was fit to fly but his wings still throbbed from his dip in the Outer Core.

"This way. It's on neutral ground," said Kitelsky. "It stands between all of our territories. It's where the three of us used to scuffle back when Mo was still out here."

"Why all the interest in Skull Rock again, anyway?" asked Putz.

"What do you mean *again*?" replied Dirk.

"Around thirty years ago the Dragnet came sniffing around asking about Minertia," said Kitelsky.

"Minertia?" said Dirk.

"Sure," replied Kitelsky. "That's where she breached the forbidden divide. We never saw nothing though, did we, Putz?"

"Not a thing," said Putz.

"And you never saw the Turning Stone?" said Dirk.

"The Turning Stone?" said Kitelsky. "So that's what this is all about. No, we never saw that."

Dirk looked up to the sky. The moon was full and the stars shone much brighter than they ever did in London. After they had been travelling a while, Kitelsky said, "Skull Rock's just past that ridge."

The three of them scaled a pile of huge boulders, then paused as they looked down on a large rock shaped like a human skull. At its base were two more dragons.

"Kinghorns," muttered Dirk. "The Mountain

Dragon's called Jegsy. The Sea Dragon is Flotsam. Vainclaw Grandin's cronies."

The two Kinghorns were using their claws to scratch away at the dirt, digging holes. "They must be searching for the Turning Stone," said Dirk.

"If they think they can come strolling into our desert, scratching around, they've got another think comin'," said Kitelsky, standing up. "You ready to rumble, Putz?"

"I sure am," said Putz.

"No," said Dirk, but it was no use. The two Desert Dragons had already spread their wings, splayed their spikes and flown down. Kitelsky landed on Flotsam's back. Putz whacked Jegsy in the face with his tail. Bursts of fire shot from the Kinghorns' mouths. Putz and Kitelsky dodged the flames and went at them again, fighting with claws and teeth.

"Idiots," said Dirk, shaking his head and staying at a safe distance.

A bubbling noise behind him caused him to spin round.

"Today I got no confusion. Today I know I got poison, so no funny business, Dirk Dilly," said Mo Sorrentino.

Dark grey smoke billowed from Dirk's nostrils but he had no desire to be on the receiving end of a face full of Desert Dragon poison.

"Where is he?" said Dirk.

"Who's the he you're referring to?" replied Sorrentino.

"Don't play games with me, Sorrentino," said Dirk. "You know who I mean – Vainclaw. I know those two are Kinghorns. I know Vainclaw's looking for the Turning Stone. I know that it was last seen out here with Minertia and I know that you aren't going to find it."

"He seems to know a lot, this one," said a low voice.

From behind a rock appeared a dragon, as dark and ominous as a shadow until the moonlight revealed his yellow belly.

"Fairfax Nordstrum," said Dirk, instantly recognizing the yellow-bellied, coal-black Cave Dweller that he had helped escape from a Dragnet cell.

"Dirk Dilly, the dragon detective. What brings you to the desert this evening?" replied Fairfax.

"So you're working for Vainclaw too?" said Dirk.

Fairfax smiled, then slinked towards Dirk. "Come, let's join the others," he said.

"One wrong move and you'll feel my poison, Dilly," said Sorrentino, remaining behind him as Fairfax led him down the rocky hill to the where Kitelsky and Putz had been clamped down by the Kinghorns.

"Get yourself off of me," said Kitelsky.

"Jegsy, I got spikes in my belly," said Flotsam.

"They're a prickly pair, ain't they?" said Jegsy, ramming Putz's head against the ground.

"Mo Sorrentino," said Kitelsky. "You double-crossin', no-good—"

"It's nothing personal," said Sorrentino. "It's just business."

"Be careful with our spiky friends," said Fairfax. "I'm sure these fine Desert Dragons will join us once we explain the situation."

"What situation?" demanded Dirk.

"First things first," replied Fairfax. "What makes you so sure we won't find the Turning Stone?"

"I went to the Inner Core," replied Dirk. "I spoke to Minertia."

Fairfax laughed. "You see, Sorrentino." He prowled

around Jegsy and Flotsam, who were still struggling to hold the Desert Dragons down. "Now that's initiative."

"I didn't need to ask. I know it's here," replied Sorrentino sharply. "She had it when she arrived but not when she left."

"And yet it doesn't seem to be here now. Maybe I should employ Mr Dilly to help me achieve my goal."

"I wouldn't take your gold, Nordstrum," snarled Dirk.

"What about power? Come and join the One-Worlders and you will be powerful," said Fairfax.

"One-Worlders," said Dirk, remembering what Karnataka had said about the Kinghorn splinter group. "So you're Vainclaw's challenger."

"Vainclaw Grandin," sneered Fairfax. "That weak fool will soon bow down before me."

Jegsy looked up from his struggle with Putz. "Never," he said, leaping off the Desert Dragon on to Fairfax's back. "Vainclaw is the true leader of the Kinghorns," he said, sinking his teeth into Fairfax's neck. Fairfax howled and lashed his tail out, sending Jegsy flying.

"I am your leader now," said the Cave Dweller, thick green blood trickling from his neck.

"I don't think so." A thundering baritone voice spoke.

Dirk spun round to see three shapes emerge from the darkness. Vainclaw Grandin approached, smoke billowing from his nose, with the two Scavenger brothers, Leon and Mali, standing either side of him.

"Hey, it's Mr Detective," said Leon.

"So it is. And hey, Jegsy," said Mali, nodding hello.

Flotsam flew angrily at Jegsy, claws thrashing. "You led Vainclaw here, didn't you?"

"You might be fine following this Cave Dweller but I'm a Grandin. Vainclaw is my leader." Jegsy shot a defensive burst of fire at him and shouted over to the Scavengers. "Leon, Mali, lend us a hand, lads."

The Scavenger brothers approached Flotsam but Kitelsky and Putz landed in front of them, rose up on to their hind legs, extended their claws and made their spikes point outwards threateningly.

"This is our territory," said Putz. "We don't want your kind around here."

"Calm down, boys," said Leon, "we got no problem with you. We just want to help our mate here."

"I don't know how you do things back home, but out here in the desert we fight fair … dragon against dragon," said Kitelsky.

"What do you say, Mali?" said Leon. "Shall we respect the local culture or what?"

"Yeah, let's snap off their spikes one by one." Mali lunged at Putz. Leon spun round, sweeping his tail across the ground, knocking Kitelsky off his feet, then diving at him. The Desert Dragons were quick and dodged the flames that the Scavengers sent their way. Behind them, Jegsy and Flotsam continued to fight viciously, tearing and scratching each other.

Dirk stepped back to avoid getting drawn into the brawl and felt something spike his tail.

"I've still got my poison," said Sorrentino.

"Aren't you going to help your friends?" said Dirk.

"I help whoever pays me," replied Sorrentino.

Also staying out of the fight were Fairfax Nordstrum and Vainclaw Grandin, standing nose to nose, maintaining eye contact. Grey smoke poured from Vainclaw's nose, intermingling with Fairfax's yellow smoke.

"You are a traitor to our species," said Fairfax.

"I will liberate our species," replied Vainclaw.

"And you do this by setting up a company in their world. You would confine humans to a life of servitude but these irritating bipeds are too spirited to work for dragons. They are too rebellious … too troublesome. Their entire history has been one of war—"

"No, their history has been one of domination," interrupted Vainclaw. "The strong control the weak."

"The only way to restore harmony to the world is to wipe out humanity," said Fairfax.

"Killing all humans would be like trying to stamp out every ant or to squash every fly. Impossible. We should conquer not annihilate," said Vainclaw. "It is I, Vainclaw Grandin, the first up-airer, who will lead all dragons to victory now."

Fairfax's eyes narrowed. He took a breath, then opened his mouth and sent black flames at Vainclaw. Dirk could feel the intense heat even from where he was standing. Vainclaw staggered back, his face blackened by the fire.

"The world isn't yours to control. It is for the One-Worlders to destroy. I am the true first up-airer. Only Minertia stood in my way and she is gone now."

"Yes, and it was I who got rid of her in the end, after she broke the forbidden divide in this very spot," said Vainclaw.

"You testified against her?" said Dirk. "But if you saw Minertia breach the forbidden divide you would have seen what she did with the Turning Stone."

Vainclaw kept his eyes focused on Fairfax but he replied to Dirk. "I may not have actually seen Minertia breach the forbidden divide but I had it on good authority from one who did. Isn't that right, Sorrentino?"

"I got nothing to say. I respect client confidentiality," said Sorrentino.

"You low life." Dirk lunged at Sorrentino, catching her off guard, knocking her over and clamping her jaw shut with his forearm.

"Get off her. She works for me now," said Fairfax, breathing black flames at Dirk, which seemed to rip through his skin and burn his bones. Dirk cried out and released Sorrentino.

"Now you're going to get it," threatened Sorrentino.

"What's that behind you?" said Dirk.

"I've seen too many films to fall for that," said Sorrentino.

"Hey, there's someone coming," said Mali.

The other dragons stopped fighting. In the darkness, two bright white lights were approaching, sending long spiky shadows across the desert landscape from the twisted Joshua trees.

"Humans," said Flotsam.

"Should we leg it?" said Jegsy.

"Kinghorns, hold your ground," ordered Vainclaw.

"The detective must have led them here," said Sorrentino.

"More like you sold the information just like you sold the film," said Dirk.

"It's of little consequence," said Fairfax. "We'll kill these humans and then settle our differences."

"On that, at least, we are agreed," replied Vainclaw.

"In the place that Minertia sealed her own fate we will seal the fate of the world," said Fairfax. "We will destroy these humans as a symbol of our intention to take back this world for all of dragonkind."

The car came to a standstill directly in front of them. The engine cut out but the lights remained on.

In their dazzling glare it was impossible to make out the figure who stepped out of the right-side door and made its way to stand in front of the beam.

"Prepare to die, human," said Vainclaw, skulking forwards.

"Oh, when you get to my age that's one thing you always have to be prepared for," said an elderly lady's voice. "My Ivor used to say that being scared of death is like being scared of cheesecake – there's really no point. Mind you, he was a silly man."

"Mrs Klingerflim?" said Dirk.

"Hello, Mr Dilly," she said. "Don't worry. I'm not here about the rent."

PROD

DIR
CAM

28

Dirk stared at his elderly landlady in disbelief. "What are you doing here?" he asked.

"Skull Rock," she sighed, looking up at the rock behind them. "Do you know, I haven't been here since I came with Ivor thirty-odd years ago."

Dirk remembered the photograph he had seen of Mrs Klingerflim and her late husband in front of the rock.

"Hey, shall we rip her head off?" said Leon.

"I would much rather you didn't. I'm quite attached to it," said Mrs Klingerflim, as the Scavengers approached.

"Not for long," threatened Mali.

Dirk needed to distract them somehow. Mrs

Klingerflim may not have been scared but he didn't like the idea of watching the sweet old lady being torn apart.

"But if you were out here dragon-spotting with Ivor, who took the photo?" he asked, skirting around the two Kinghorns, putting himself in a position where, if need be, he could throw himself in front of Mrs Klingerflim.

Mrs Klingerflim smiled warmly. "You are clever, Mr Dilly. You've guessed, haven't you?"

"And that scratch on the lens?" said Dirk.

"Well, she had very big claws. It's a wonder she could operate the camera at all."

"Who? What are you talking about?" said Vainclaw.

"Minertia." Mrs Klingerflim's eyes widened. "She was the biggest, oldest and wisest dragon of them all. We were out here to spot these lovely Desert Dragons. I used to love watching you play-fighting," she said, waving at Putz and Kitelsky.

"Watchin' us?" said Kitelsky.

"Play-fightin'?" said Putz.

"Then on the third day we heard a voice. She spoke in our heads, I remember. We turned round and there

she was, as big as a mountain. I shall never forget it."
Mrs Klingerflim wiped a tear from her eye.

"So she approached you?" said Dirk.

"Yes, it turned out she'd been watching us for some time, checking we were the right sort of people."

"The right sort of people for what?" said Vainclaw.

"A reconciliation," replied Mrs Klingerflim. "She believed that the time had come for dragons to come out of hiding. She told us she thought she had made a mistake at the conference only giving dragonkind a choice between hiding and fighting. She dreamed of a world where humans and dragons could live side by side."

"Impossible," said Vainclaw.

"We thought it was a splendid idea. We were young then, well, younger than now, at least. We thought we could change the world, help dragons come out of hiding and live in harmony with humans."

The dragons stood captivated, listening to the old lady.

"The Summit of Skull Rock," said Dirk.

"That's what Ivor called it in some article he wrote. He did like to make things sound grand. It was just the three of us having a natter, really."

"What happened to the Turning Stone?" asked Sorrentino.

Mrs Klingerflim took her glasses off, wiped them and placed them back. "I remember you," she said, peering at the Desert Dragon. "You saw us. Minertia called out to you to join us but you ran away."

"She had the Turning Stone when she arrived but not when she left. Where did she hide it?" asked Sorrentino.

"I'm afraid it's not anywhere any more, my dear," said Mrs Klingerflim.

"What do you mean?" asked Vainclaw.

"She destroyed it," replied the old lady.

"She destroyed it?" said Fairfax Nordstrum, the yellow smoke from his nostrils darkening.

"Oh, you're a coal-black, yellow-bellied Cave Dweller, aren't you?" she said, turning to look at him. "You're the first one I've ever seen."

"And I'll be the last if you don't answer me. Why did she destroy it?" said Fairfax.

"She said that it could too easily end up with the wrong sort of dragon," said Mrs Klingerflim. "So she put it between her teeth and split it into pieces. I took one of the bits as a souvenir. It makes a lovely paperweight."

"And now we shall put you between our teeth and split *you* into pieces," said Vainclaw.

"Hey, boss, wait, the old girl's not alone," said Mali, who had noticed something else in the darkness. Dirk turned to see that another set of headlights was approaching.

Brant Buchanan had said very little on the way. He sat next to Weaver as the car headed out of the city. Archie, Holly and Callum were trapped in the back, unable to escape.

The roads were quieter and darker out here. The night sky looked pale in comparison. Holly and Archie tried pressing every button in the high-tech car but nothing worked. Callum remained huddled in a corner, with a look of wild mania in his eyes. The car turned on to a bumpy track, passing strangely shaped trees silhouetted against the sky until the headlights caught sight of something more unusual.

"I can't make out what I'm looking at," said Archie.

"Dragons," said Holly.

"Yes. See anyone you recognize?" said Buchanan as they neared.

Holly didn't respond but Callum said, "Vainclaw."

"Isn't that Mrs Klin—" Archie was cut short by Holly putting her hand over his mouth, not wanting Brant Buchanan to learn any more than he already knew.

The car stopped in front of the incredible scene and, after a moment, Buchanan and Weaver got out.

"Dirk!" screamed Holly, but the doors slammed shut and the locks clicked.

Trapped in the soundproofed car, Holly, Archie and Callum were unable to hear what they were saying.

PROD

29

DIR
CAM

Weaver slowed down as he approached the dragons and turned to look at his boss. "Are you sure about this?" he asked out of the corner of his mouth.

Brant Buchanan's eyes remained transfixed on the dragons. "There's always a little risk in business," he replied.

"Yes, sir, but still..."

Working for a man like Buchanan, Weaver was accustomed to hostile environments. You didn't get to Buchanan's position without making a few enemies on the way. In the past Weaver had dealt with bitter former employees, angry competitors and even the occasional crook with a plan to kidnap his employer for the ransom. In every one of these instances Weaver had assessed the risk and executed the necessary measures to keep Mr Buchanan from harm.

In the current situation, being in the middle of the desert with an unidentified car, ten rather vicious-looking dragons and an elderly lady, he had already established that the safest thing to do would be to turn the car round and drive quickly away. Unfortunately, Buchanan had already ruled out that option.

On the plus side, working for one of the richest men in the world had its advantages. Weaver pulled back his sleeve and clutched his watch.

Buchanan glanced at him. "Looking for an opportunity to play with your new toy?"

"Actually I'm hoping I won't have to," he replied.

"Remember they have soft bellies," said Buchanan.

"They also have lethal claws, razor-sharp teeth and the ability to breathe fire," replied Weaver.

Buchanan grinned. "That too."

"That's far enough," said a dragon that the billionaire recognized at once.

"Dirk Dilly," he replied. "At last we meet in the flesh." He turned to the largest Mountain Dragon.

"And would I be right in thinking that this is Callum's play pal, Vainclaw Grandin?"

Vainclaw reared up on to his hind legs, then landed heavily back on all fours and remained where he was. "Soon you will only speak my name when begging for mercy, human," he snarled.

"We could go down that route," said Buchanan, "or we could find another way through this."

"We'll toast him and roast him," said Jegsy.

Jegsy, Leon and Mali stepped forwards and opened their jaws.

Weaver pressed down on his watch, causing it to suddenly expand to the size of a shield. The two watch hands grew larger too. In a swift movement, Weaver pulled off the big hand, which was now the size of a sword.

Jegsy and Leon sent two mouthfuls of flames at him, but Weaver held up his shield, protecting him and his boss. As the flames subsided, he leaped forwards with his sword extended. The sword fizzed with some kind of electrical current. He thrust it at Jegsy, catching his claw and sending the dragon flying.

"Don't hurt them." Mrs Klingerflim rushed forwards, but Weaver pushed her away. She landed facedown between the two cars.

"Mrs K!" said Dirk, diving to help her.

There was no response.

"Stand back!" Weaver nervously pointed the sword at Dirk. "Unless you want to be on the receiving end of a thousand volts of electricity."

"Ah, the brave knight slays the dragon and knocks the elderly lady over in the dirt," replied Dirk.

"I said stand back," repeated Weaver.

"And I said no."

Dirk moved to help Mrs Klingerflim again, but Weaver panicked and thrust the sword at him. Dirk tried to avoid it but the sharp tip of the sword connected with his neck and sent a surge of deadly electricity through him. He tried to defend himself with fire, but Weaver blocked it with the shield and pushed the sword deeper into his flesh, lighting him up from inside.

"I think you've made your point," said Buchanan.

Weaver retracted the sword.

Dirk lay slumped on the ground. Green blood

seeped out, forming a pool on the dusty desert floor around where his body lay.

"You see, my scaly friends, the classic dragon-fighting kit has come a long way since the Middle Ages," said Brant Buchanan. "The shield produces a heat-resistant electromagnetic forcefield, while the sword can defeat the strongest of your species."

"Your toys do not frighten us and killing this detective just saves me a job. What have you got to say to us?" said Vainclaw in his deep baritone.

"I've come to make a deal," Buchanan replied.

"What sort of deal?" asked Vainclaw.

Fairfax shook his head. "True Kinghorns do not make deals with humans. They destroy them."

"We will be their masters," said Vainclaw.

The two dragons snarled at each other.

"Destroy, defeat…" said Buchanan. "I offer a third option."

"Speak," said Vainclaw.

"Why divide the world between dragons and humans when we can divide it between the strong and the weak, regardless of species?"

Much to Weaver's agitation, his boss had walked

up to the two dragons and was standing between them as they listened to what he was saying. Weaver raised his sword and shield again.

"And believe me," continued Buchanan, "I am strong. I have technology and weaponry that will ensure our victory. Together, having conquered all those who stand in our way, we will rule this planet, dragon and man united by strength."

The two dragons looked at each other, sending clouds of black and yellow smoke into Buchanan's face.

"It's an interesting proposition," said Vainclaw.

"The predator does not negotiate with his prey," said Fairfax.

"Sir," said Weaver anxiously.

"Don't worry, Weaver," said Buchanan.

But Weaver was looking at the claws that both dragons had extended. He was watching the other dragons as they gathered round.

"You have been most persuasive," said Vainclaw, edging nearer to Buchanan.

"Dragons have methods of persuasion too." Fairfax shifted his fearsome face close to Buchanan's.

"Both of you, stand back," shouted Weaver, holding his sword out.

"Relax, Weaver," said Buchanan.

But Weaver didn't feel relaxed. The dragons that surrounded his boss were looking like they could strike at any moment. He needed to warn them not to try anything. He lifted his shield in front of his face and swung his sword from side to side. He increased the voltage to maximum. The equipment had been developed for this purpose but it had never been tested before. The shield was designed not just to protect from the heat but also from sound, although Buchanan hadn't explained why. This was disconcerting because it meant that, for a moment, all sound cut out. Weaver lowered the shield to assess the situation and was surprised to discover that no one was moving. Every one of the dragons – and Brant Buchanan himself – was standing exactly as they had been, frozen, with a faraway look in their eyes.

30

Locked inside the car, Holly and Archie cried out when Weaver knocked Mrs Klingerflim to the ground. They screamed when he lunged at Dirk. Holly banged the window, tears streaming down her face. Archie gripped the door handle so hard his knuckles went white. Callum sat huddled in a corner, mumbling to himself.

As the car was fully soundproofed, they didn't hear anything that was said but they did witness something the others failed to notice. While Buchanan had the full attention of the dragons, a shadowy figure appeared by Mrs Klingerflim's side. The man's face was obscured by a wide-brimmed hat but Holly still recognized him.

"It's Ladbroke Blake," she said. "What's he doing here?"

Unseen by the others, Ladbroke lifted Mrs Klingerflim and carried her to her car. And then…

… everyone froze.

Everyone except for Weaver.

"What's happened?" asked Archie.

"One of them must have used Dragonsong."

"But which one?" asked Archie.

"I don't know. We've got to get out. If only we could break the—" She stopped. "Of course." She reached inside her T-shirt and pulled out the dragon claw she wore around her neck. "Dragon claws can cut through anything."

Holly jammed the claw into the side of the door. There was a crunch as it cut through the lock and then the door swung open.

"Vainclaw. He's not moving." Callum sprung up and pushed past them, running to the Mountain Dragon's side. Holly and Archie rushed to Dirk's unmoving body and fell to their knees.

"Try to push him over," said Holly but, as much as they tried, they couldn't move him.

"You need a hand with that?" said a voice behind them. Holly spun round to see the familiar weather-beaten face that always had a habit of turning up when she most needed him. She hugged him, then said, "Archie, this is Ladbroke, the detective I told you about." She turned back to him and said, "What are you doing here?"

"Let's get this dragon on his back first."

Weaver, who had been trying to wake up Mr Buchanan, turned round and said, "What's happened to him?"

"Never mind him, give me a hand," snapped Ladbroke.

Together, Weaver and Ladbroke pushed Dirk on to his back.

"I'm sorry, Holly. It looks bad," said Ladbroke.

Holly forced herself to look. Weaver's sword had made a hole in his neck and he had lost a fair amount of blood, but the electrical surge of the sword had torn through him and left his scales looking charred and cracked. Holly fell to her knees and collapsed into tears, her hands across his belly. "Oh, Dirk," she cried. "Please say something."

"I'm sorry," said Weaver quietly.

Holly didn't register his words. She felt Dirk's blood fill the gaps between her fingers. She raised her head, looking at the stars, blurry through her teary eyes. This was the end, she thought. He was dead. Dirk was dead. After all she had been through with Dirk, protecting mankind from the Kinghorns, it was a human weapon that had killed him.

Killed.

Dead.

The words lost their meanings as Holly wept.

The pain in her heart was so overwhelming that she barely noticed the dull ache in her leg. But it was insistent. It came from the bone fixed by the Sky Dragon, Nebula Colorado. It felt as if the bone was trying to tell her something.

She remembered Nebula's words – *Part of me is now a part of you* – and suddenly she knew what to do. She didn't know how. She hadn't heard a voice or seen a vision. She simply knew as though she had always known.

"All of you, hold him down," she said, wiping her eyes, smearing green blood across her cheek.

"Holly, he's gone," said Ladbroke gently.

"Hold him down," repeated Holly. "You too, Weaver."

"What's happened to Mr Buchanan?" said Weaver.

"Do as she says!" shouted Archie.

Weaver looked like he wanted to say something, but he placed the shield and sword on the ground, sat down and held Dirk's tail. Ladbroke took his head and Archie held his wings. Callum remained where he was, stroking Vainclaw's paw and muttering, "My monster, my monster."

Holly placed her hands over the gash where the blade had entered. She felt the torn flesh and the open arteries between her fingers. She concentrated hard and felt warming energy spread from her leg and fill her body. She allowed that ancient healing energy to spill out through her fingertips and into Dirk's torn, broken body, repairing and healing. By the time she had removed her palms, the wound had healed over.

"How did you do that?" Archie said.

"I don't know," she said. "Is it enough?"

Dirk's body twitched. He let out a low moan.

"Just enough, kiddo," he muttered.

PROD
31
DIR
CAM

Dirk had once seen a TV show in which people described their near-death experiences. Most of them had described the usual tunnels with white lights at the end. As Dirk felt Weaver's blade do its terrible work and his life force ebb away, he hadn't seen anything, but in the darkness he had heard something. At first it was just garbled noise, then he heard a voice he hadn't heard for a long time. It was his mother. He could hear the first words she had ever spoken to him, the first words he had ever heard, as he crawled from the Outer Core as a youngling. At the time he had been too young to understand but now, as the words came back, he heard her say, *There, there, little one, you have finished the hardest journey.*

The voice grew fainter.

Then he heard another.

It was Minertia.

You have many adventures ahead of you before you need to worry about that. Keep your secrets for now.

He heard more voices – some of them he remembered. Others were new. They spoke over each other, growing louder and louder until suddenly, the voices disappeared, leaving silence – peaceful, endless silence – and Dirk knew that this was the end. This was death.

Then, in the dark nothingness, one quiet voice spoke.

"Dirk! Come back to me." He felt human arms around his neck.

Dirk opened his eyes and raised his head. "What happened?" he said.

"You got a little slayed," said a man in a wide-brimmed hat.

"Ladbroke Blake?" Dirk lifted himself up and examined his blood-smeared belly.

"Dirk Dilly," replied the craggy-faced man, smiling.

"It was you who rescued us from the library,"

he said. "But how…"

"Enough," said Weaver, picking up his sword and jumping to his feet. "What is wrong with Mr Buchanan?"

"The same thing that's wrong with all of them," said Dirk. "They're under the spell of Dragonsong."

"But whose?" said Holly.

"I don't know," said Dirk.

"As far as I could tell from the car, both dragons sang," said Ladbroke.

"They must have done it at precisely the same time and entranced each other as well as everyone else," said Dirk.

"But how do we get him out of it?" asked Weaver.

"Like this." Ladbroke slapped Buchanan hard in his face. The billionaire rocked with the force. He blinked, then looked at Weaver with a vacant smile.

"Mr Buchanan, sir," Weaver said. "Are you all right?"

"The monsters and the music… Did you hear the music? It sounded like the sound of forever. Did you see the monsters? They've gone now but they were here."

"What are you talking about, sir?" said Weaver. "What's wrong with him?"

"I don't know," said Ladbroke. "That should have worked."

"Pretty music in my head and monsters in my hair," sang Brant Buchanan, ruffling his silver hair.

Dirk approached but Buchanan stared straight through him and said, "All the monsters have gone now."

Dirk lifted a paw and slapped him again.

Buchanan swayed and said, "Where did the music go? Did the monsters take it with them?"

"It's like he's still under," said Holly.

"Look at the positioning," said Dirk. "Vainclaw and Fairfax were on either side of Buchanan. He was directly in between both Dragonsongs. He got a double dose. It must have damaged his brain in some way."

"Is there a cure?" said Weaver.

"I don't know. I've never heard of it happening before," said Dirk. "Why didn't it affect you?"

"The shield cuts out sound," said Weaver. "We learned about Dragonsong from the book so we included noise cancellation as a feature."

"Then I should sing and make you forget now," said Dirk.

"There is no need. Believe me, I have no interest in any of this. Let me take Mr Buchanan back. He needs medical attention. You have my word that I'll destroy his evidence and do my best to keep him away from dragons in the future. I've never liked this project."

"I can't see that we have much choice," said Dirk.

Buchanan staggered over to where Callum was crouched at Vainclaw's feet, stroking his legs.

"Where is the music?" he said to the boy.

"I've heard it too. My monster used to sing to me, now he hears it himself," replied Callum.

"The monsters have gone," said Buchanan.

"The monsters are all around us," replied Callum.

"Take the boy back too," said Dirk. "Send him back to his father."

Weaver took Callum and Buchanan by the hand and led them to the car, then looked back.

"I don't want my stepmum to work for Mr Buchanan any more," said Holly.

Weaver nodded. "I'll make sure she gets a fair redundancy deal."

"Make sure you destroy all the evidence," called Ladbroke.

Weaver nodded, got in the car and started the engine. The others watched the car disappear into the darkness.

Then Archie said, "Who did you say you were?"

"His name is Ladbroke—" Holly began.

"Actually, my *real* name is Pi."

"Pie?"

"Pi Blandford."

He held up a card for them all to see.

AGENT PI BLANDFORD

International Agency of Investigations into
Unusual Occurrences

"You're not called Ladbroke?" said Holly.

"If it helps, Ladbroke is my preferred alias," he said.

"And you know about dragons?" said Holly.

"Technically, no, the agency doesn't know anything about anything," said Ladbroke, "because the things we investigate do not technically exist."

"Isn't that a bit weird?" said Archie.

"What's weirder? Pretending dragons don't exist or knowing that they do?" said Ladbroke.

"So you knew right from the beginning?" Holly said.

"When I first got assigned responsibility for dragons, I found a copy of Mr Klingerflim's book. I decided to check out his widow's house. That was when I discovered Dirk. When I saw you go in, Holly, I followed you home. Listening in on your phone conversations I learned that your stepmother wanted to hire someone to follow you so I made sure that she found another of my cards."

Ladbroke held out a cream-coloured card that read:

LADBROKE BLAKE
BLAKE INVESTIGATIONS
Confidential, Professional and Affordable
Private Investigations

"Why have you never let on you knew before?" said Holly.

"The agency has a policy of non-intervention. I'm not supposed to get involved. My job is only to collect information on dragons."

"Well, I'd hardly call this non-intervention, Mr Blandford. You're surrounded by dragons and you're talking to one," said an elderly female voice behind him.

"Mrs Klingerflim!" said Holly, running to help the old lady out of the car and noticing the nasty purple bruise under her eye.

"Hello, dear. Hello, Archie. Hello, Mr Dilly."

"So Ladbroke brought you here?" said Dirk.

"He was kind enough to fly me over," said Mrs Klingerflim. "We only arrived today, didn't we, Mr Blandford?"

"I wanted to know why Buchanan had brought Holly to Los Angeles," said Ladbroke. "I did a little research and learned about the Summit of Skull Rock. There were no details in our case files, except for the names of those involved – Ivor and Elsita Klingerflim."

"Elsita?" said Holly.

"That's my name, dear," said Mrs Klingerflim. "You didn't think my first name was Mrs, did you?"

Ladbroke continued. "I learned that Buchanan was

turning his library into some kind of trap. When the substation went down, I dropped by and opened the roof. I never had any direct contact with the dragons, so I didn't really break any rules."

"Is that why you left Mrs Klingerflim to get out of the car and confront the Kinghorns on her own?" asked Dirk.

"No," said Mrs Klingerflim. "I told Mr Blandford to stay inside in case they used Dragonsong."

"But what about you?" asked Holly.

"Me? I was rather hoping to hear it." She smiled wistfully. "I heard it once. Minertia sang for Ivor and me. It was beautiful."

"I think we should be dealing with our present predicament," said Ladbroke. "Mr Dilly, I'd appreciate your thoughts. How do we clean this up?" He gesticulated to the nine dragons, standing as motionless as models in a theme park.

"Leave them to me," said Dirk. "Will you make sure Holly and Archie get home safely?"

"The whole family will be flown home courtesy of the agency."

"I owe you my life, kiddo," Dirk said to Holly.

Dirk had never been a big hugger. Hugging wasn't really something dragons did and Dirk had always struggled to understand why humans were so keen on squeezing each other. But when Holly threw her arms round him, that moment was so full of love, warmth and gratitude that Dirk felt as though he finally understood.

"When will we see you next?" said Holly.

"Very soon."

"It's been a pleasure never having met you, Mr Dilly," said Ladbroke, shaking Dirk's paw.

After saying his goodbyes, Dirk watched the cars drive away into the darkness, then turned to look at the three Desert Dragons, the two Scavenger brothers, the Sea Dragon, Vainclaw, his nephew, Jegsy, and the yellow-bellied, coal-black Cave Dweller, all frozen with the same faraway look in their eyes.

"Fairfax Nordstrum," said Dirk, looking at him. "Don't worry, you'll be back behind bars soon enough. Only this time, I'll have a word with Captain Karnataka and make sure you're convicted alongside these other Kinghorns." Dirk looked at the rest of the dragons. "I know none of you can hear a word I'm saying now but, in a minute, you will. After I've sung a little Dragonsong you'll all do exactly as I say when I tell you to turn yourselves in."

Dirk stood back and opened his mouth to sing. He hesitated. So many good dragons had lost their lives because of Dragonsong, he hated it. It was against the law to use it as a weapon, but he could think of no other way of resolving the situation.

Nine dragons stood frozen in front of him.

Nine sets of yellow eyes stared blankly ahead.

Then one set blinked.

Before Dirk could react, Fairfax Nordstrum's mouth opened and he felt a burning sensation as black flames shot out. The Cave Dweller leaped forwards and landed forcefully on top of Dirk, his claws digging into his skin.

"Here's something interesting," he said in a low voice. "Did you know that the older the dragon, the shorter the effects of Dragonsong last? I'm guessing not, otherwise you may have cut your speech. I'm an old dragon, Mr Dilly."

Dirk wrestled a leg free and kicked Fairfax off him, leaping up and diving at him, claws drawn. Fairfax evaded his attack and swung his tail at Dirk, but

Dirk rolled out of the way and the tail smacked into Sorrentino's face, knocking her out of her stupor. Dirk jumped to his feet but was too slow. Fairfax was on top of him, pinning him down.

"So, Dirk Dilly, dragon detective," said Fairfax. "Traitor to your species. My dark fire will melt your pathetic brain. Do you have any last words?"

Dirk looked into Fairfax's cruel yellow eyes. He could feel the heat from his breath but he was helpless to stop him. "Dying twice in one night, lucky me," he said. "I guess it's true, the bad guys do get their fair share of winning too."

"Sorrentino, come and watch me kill this dragon," said Fairfax. "Sorrentino?"

Suddenly Fairfax's face contorted with pain. He let out a scream that filled the empty desert.

Dirk felt the weight lift off him as Fairfax fell to the ground, screaming, writhing in agony and lashing out in desperation. "What is this?" he cried.

Dirk stood up and saw on Fairfax's black back a patch of sticky green liquid hissing, burning its way through his thick scaly skin. Behind him, Sorrentino wiped her mouth.

"Thank you," said Dirk. "But I thought you worked for him."

"I'm off the clock," replied Sorrentino. "Besides, I like my life just the way it is. I don't need no Kinghorn messing things up, starting wars."

Fairfax writhed in agony as the poison tore through his body. He lashed out, limbs flying in all directions, catching Leon with his tail, sending him smacking into his brother who, in turn, barged into Jegsy and Flotsam, waking them all up.

"Boss, what's wrong?" said Flotsam.

"Help me!" shouted Fairfax.

"Come on, boss." Flotsam grabbed Fairfax and dragged him on to a large piece of flat rock. He uttered a few words in Dragonspeak and the rock drew the two of them down, closing over their heads, muffling the sound of Fairfax's screams.

Jegsy awoke Vainclaw with a smack in the face. The Mountain Dragon looked around. "I don't know what's happened here," he said with a deep growl, "but now let us finally rid ourselves of this turbulent detective."

Dirk stepped back, trying to work out the best way to fight the four dragons. The Kinghorns advanced.

"I don't think so," said Sorrentino, leaping over them and landing next to Dirk.

"I'll make it worth your while not to get involved in this, Sorrentino," said Vainclaw.

Sorrentino held her ground.

"Very well, we will destroy you both," said Vainclaw.

"I thought I already explained that out here in the desert we fight fair," said Kitelsky. He and Putz landed next to Dirk and Sorrentino, claws drawn, spikes splayed.

Vainclaw sent a burst of fire forwards and the Kinghorns attacked, but this time the Desert Dragons worked as a team. Putz grabbed on to Kitelsky's forelegs and swung him round, smacking Leon and Mali sideways. While they were still reeling, Sorrentino flew over and came down hard on Vainclaw's head. Jegsy tried to help his boss but Putz swiped him with a claw. Leon roared fire at Sorrentino but she ducked and the fire caught Mali straight in the face.

"Watch it, bro," said Mali.

Vainclaw attempted to send another burst of fire at Sorrentino, but Putz was on him, jabbing his claws into his back.

In fact the Desert Dragons were fighting so well, instinctively reading each other's moves, working together, that Dirk stepped back from the fight and watched. The Kinghorns were losing ground. It was only a matter of time before Vainclaw cried, "Kinghorns, retreat! We'll save this fight for another day."

Finally defeated, Vainclaw and the Kinghorns ran to the rocks, spoke quickly and vanished into the ground.

"Nice job," said Dirk.

"Now, that's what I call a rumble," said Kitelsky.

33

The return flight to England was distinctly less glamorous than the private jet that had taken Holly and Archie there. Ladbroke had pulled some strings to get around Archie's lack of passport but, instead of Buchanan's luxury jet, they took an ordinary plane full of people, crammed in like sardines.

"I still don't understand why Brant made you redundant," said Mr Bigsby, moving his elbow out of the way of the stewardess, who was coming down the aisle with the duty-free trolley.

"After speaking to him, I think I'm better off out," said Mrs Bigsby. "Besides, the redundancy money will provide plenty of exciting opportunities."

Holly and Archie were sitting behind them. The

seatbelt sign went off and they twisted round to kneel on their seats. Behind them Mrs Klingerflim was snoozing next to Ladbroke Blake. He leaned forwards and said quietly, "She fell asleep as soon as we sat down."

"Will she be OK? It was a nasty fall," said Holly.

"Don't worry. She's tougher than she looks. I wouldn't be surprised if she has a little dragon blood in her too. But I'll keep an eye on her," replied Ladbroke.

"What I don't get," said Archie, "is that Buchanan said he got the idea to set a trap when he heard Holly talking about the film, but wasn't it his idea to steal the film in the first place?"

"No," said Ladbroke. "Chase Lampton hired Sorrentino."

"Chase? Why?" said Holly.

"He knew that the movie was going badly and the studio had told him that if he made one more flop they were going to drop him. He had a problem, so he phoned Sorrentino for a solution. Sorrentino told him to take his cameras to the desert."

"But how would a film of dragons help?" said Archie.

"From what I've gathered, Chase believed that

people in Hollywood are easily distracted. His plan was to reveal the footage the same week that Petal's film was released, and while everyone was inviting him on chat shows to talk about dragons, Petal's film would go unnoticed."

"Would that really have worked?" asked Holly doubtfully.

"Who knows? But I can see how people might be more interested in the fact there are dragons in the desert than in a film about a popstar's daughter. Eventually, Chase planned to reveal that the whole thing was an elaborate hoax, by which time he would already be making his next film and everyone would be left wondering how he made such realistic special effects. I think he was hoping to get an action movie off the back of it."

"But it wasn't a hoax," said Archie. "The dragons were real."

"Chase didn't know that." Ladbroke poured himself a drink. "He thought Sorrentino was giving him a brilliant fake. He never dreamed that the footage would be real."

"What if someone went looking for them in the

desert?" asked Holly.

"Sorrentino would have told Putz and Kitelsky to hide out until the whole thing blew over."

"So, if Sorrentino was doing it for Chase, who stole the film?" asked Archie.

"Sorrentino," said Ladbroke. "When no one was looking, she decided to take the film so she could charge Chase more for it."

"But she didn't sell it to Chase?" said Holly.

"No, she got a better offer," replied Ladbroke, opening a packet of nuts and chucking a couple into his mouth. "After hearing you telling Dirk about it on the phone, Buchanan instructed Precious and Frank to acquire the film, whatever the cost. Then Sorrentino got greedy. She sold it to them for loads more money than Chase was willing to pay."

"Chase can't have been happy."

"He wasn't. So Sorrentino promised to do the only thing left to save Petal's film. She set fire to the rushes."

"But won't they just make it again?" said Archie.

"No. After all the bad publicity, World Studios has decided to leave it. The funny thing is that it turns out because of the insurance pay out, *Petal: The Movie* is

Chase's biggest success in years financially. He's already got a new film in production. Something about alien cats living on earth." Ladbroke snorted with laughter.

Holly and Archie laughed too.

"Talking of films –" Ladbroke pulled a set of headphones from a plastic bag – "if you don't mind, I'm going to watch a movie. I'll speak to you later."

Holly and Archie sat back down in their seats and flicked through the films on offer.

"What do you fancy watching?" asked Archie.

Holly looked at the options. "Hey, *The Big Zero*," she said. "That's the one Dirk said was Chase's best film. Let's see what it's like."

They both put on their headphones and the opening music began.

Soon they would arrive back in London and they would have to deal with school and all the other bits of reality they had avoided thinking about on holiday. But for the moment they lost themselves in the film.

The screen showed an aerial view of Los Angeles. The camera moved in and a gruff voice spoke over the music.

"In some stories, the kind they like to tell you in

Hollywood, the good guys always win and the bad guys always lose. Well, I live in the real Hollywood and I can tell you that in real life it ain't like that. In my experience, the bad guys get their fair share of winning too."

Holly thought of Dirk and how she had almost lost him. She wondered how he was getting home.

The white shutter was pulled over the window, otherwise she might have noticed, if she had looked very carefully, the tip of a claw belonging to a four-metre-long (from nose to tail), red-backed, green-bellied, urban-based Mountain Dragon, clinging to the top of the plane, perfectly blended with its paintwork, enjoying the free ride back home.

Turn the page to read Dirk and
Holly's first adventure in...

A MISSING CAT...
A TRAIL OF CLUES...
A DETECTIVE
DREAM TEAM!

DRAGON
DETECTIVE

MISSING

CATNAPPED!
GARETH P. JONES

Dirk Dilly reclined with his feet resting on his desk, watching the smoke curl up from his mouth and fill the room. It spiralled up and then, as it caught in a breeze coming through the window, swooped back down. Business was slow. If the truth be told, he wasn't sure how long he'd been sat there. Two hours? Three? He could turn his head to look at the clock but it all seemed like so much effort. Anyway, he had never quite got to grips with telling the time. It was such a peculiar method of measuring things. Sixty seconds in a minute. Sixty minutes in an hour. Twenty-four hours in a day. He understood the principle, all right. It just seemed like a funny way to chop up time.

Dirk listened to the traffic passing and closed

his eyes. He felt so relaxed that when the phone rang, harshly breaking the trance he was in, he fell backwards, his long, scaly tail lashing out, knocking the clock clean off the wall. It smashed on the floor.

"Rats!" he growled, with such force that a small, thin line of fire darted from his mouth. The flames caught a pile of yellowing newspapers that Dirk hadn't got around to filing yet, setting them alight.

"Big rats!" he said, springing to his feet. He threw the contents of his glass of neat orange squash at the spreading fire. It was woefully inadequate. The fire reached the curtains. Dirk looked around in panic. In the corner of the room was an old fire extinguisher. He whipped out his tail to grab it but, rather than latching on properly, his tail caught the pull cord, immediately setting it off. White foam shot across the room and the extinguisher spun around, covering everything in sight. Everything, that was, except the fire, which was now blackening the ceiling.

"Big, fat rats!"

There was only one thing for it. The painful option. He flapped his wings a couple of times and lifted himself into the air. Then, wincing in anticipation of the pain, he threw himself against the curtains and ceiling. The whole building shook and Dirk landed heavily on his desk. He lifted his head and looked up. The fire was out. There was a moment's pause before the pain registered.

"Owwww!" he groaned.

His scaly, red back was fireproof but he had landed with some force on his soft, green underbelly, which was now making an alarming ringing noise.

"I must have hurt myself pretty bad," he muttered worriedly. "What does a ringing belly mean?"

Tentatively he lifted himself up on his four legs to examine the damage. The ringing grew louder. He took a deep breath and looked down. To his great relief he found he had been lying on the telephone. He climbed off the desk and sat down behind it, catching his breath before answering.

"The Dragon Detective Agency. Dirk Dilly speaking."

"Hello, are you a detective?" It was a human child, a girl, by the pitch of the voice.

"How old are you?"

"Eleven. Why?"

"That's too young. Goodbye." Dirk put the phone down.

Kids, he thought. *Time wasters*. And that was that.

Or rather that would have been that had the phone not started ringing again. In actual fact, *that* was going to be anything but *that*. By picking up the phone for a second time he made sure that *that* was about as far from *that* as was humanly – or even dragonly – possible.

"Hello?" said the girl's voice again.

"What do you want, kid?" he said gruffly.

"My cat's been stolen."

"I don't do animals."

On the other end of the phone there came a strange gurgling-hiccupping-wailing noise. She was crying.

"Listen," said Dirk, a little softness creeping into his voice in spite of himself.

But the noise kept coming.

"Listen," he said more sternly.

The girl still sobbed.

"All right! I'll find your cat."

The crying stopped suddenly and the voice said with surprising brightness, "Great. My address is forty-three Elliot Drive. The cat's name is Willow."

"And have your parents looked for the cat?" he asked.

"I'm not even sure they know we have a cat," she replied.

"Why do you think it's been stolen?"

"Because Willow always comes in when I call her but she didn't tonight."

"Tonight? When did you last see her?"

"This morning."

"So she's been missing for how long?"

"I normally call her for dinner at about four o'clock."

Dirk glanced at the space on his wall where the clock should have been, then looked down to where it lay on the floor. He flipped it over with his tail. It had stopped with the big hand pointing at the six, and the smaller halfway between the four and the five. If he wasn't mistaken, it was half past four.

"You're telling me that your cat has been missing for thirty minutes and you've called me?"

"I told you. She always comes when I call her."

"Hey, kiddo, I'm going to put the phone down. Don't call me again. Don't even think about it.

Don't even think about thinking it. If you even think about thinking about thinking about... Where was I?"

But the girl didn't answer. Instead the awful noise started again, growing louder and louder like an air-raid siren. Dirk wasn't exactly soft-hearted and he had no love of humans, let alone their small, annoying offspring, but the noise was so horrible that he knew that even if he put the receiver down the memory of it would linger on. And so, against every molecule of common sense in his large, scaly body, he put the phone back to his long, pointy ear and said, "All right. I'll check it out."

"Great," said the girl cheerfully. "My name is Holly, by the way. Holly Bigsby."

After getting the cat's description, Dirk put the phone down and prepared to leave. It wasn't his usual sort of work. Normally he located lost items, tracked down troublesome teenagers or took photos of people off work with 'bad backs' who were actually taking trampolining holidays.

He slipped his notebook behind his wing and peeked though the slatted blinds. Satisfied that no one was looking, he pulled the cord and opened the window. What could be simpler than a missing cat? It was probably stuck up a tree or had found a woman next door with fuller fat milk or maybe it had been run over. No, this would be an easy case. He spread his wings, flapped them a couple of times and leaped out.

You may be wondering what a dragon was doing working in London as a private detective. The answer is that if you're going to be a private detective, London is a large city with lots of people with lots of problems, so there's plenty of work to be had.

The other advantage of London for your average jobbing dragon is that hardly anyone ever looks up, which means that even if you are a four-metre-long, red-backed, green-bellied, urban-based Mountain Dragon, as long as you stick to roofs no one's ever going to see you.

Of course, there had been some close calls. But even if someone did look up in the middle of Piccadilly Circus and catch a glimpse of a medium-sized dragon passing overhead, by the time they had blinked or rubbed their eyes or tapped their husband on the arm to say, "Look, a medium-sized dragon just flew past," Dirk was safely out of sight.

And the husband would say something like, "A dragon? In London? Don't be ridiculous."

And his wife might reply, "That's what I saw."

And he would say, "Maybe it floated over from Chinatown. They have big paper dragons for Chinese New Year."

And she would say, "When is Chinese New Year?"

And so on until one of them would say something along the lines of, "We haven't had Chinese food for ages. Let's have some tonight. Mmmm … sweet-and-sour pork." And the memory of seeing a dragon would vanish as quickly as the dragon had himself.

While having to remain unseen would be inconvenient for a teacher or a bank clerk or an insurance salesman, it is an undeniable advantage for a private detective. Dirk only ever spoke to clients over the phone. In fact the only face-to-face interaction he ever had with humans was with his elderly landlady, Mrs Klingerflim, who lived below his office. Although she claimed to be able to see perfectly well through her thick glasses, her eyesight was clearly much worse than she let on. Dirk had discovered this when she walked into his office and caught him asleep, head slumped over his desk.

"Oh, I am so sorry," she had said as she opened the door.

Dirk had awoken with a start. "Er, Mrs Klingerflim. I-I can explain," he said, ducking behind the desk.

"No need, Mr Dilly. After all, your rent is only two days late. I just wanted to remind you in case you'd forgotten," said the sweet old lady.

"My rent? Oh my rent…" he had replied. Then, testing the water, he had stood up again and said, "I meant to apologize for my appearance."

She looked him up and down and said, "I think you look fine, Mr Dilly. Very smart. My Ivor never looked smart in his life. On our wedding day, the vicar threw him out of the church. He thought he was a homeless person who had come in for the wine!"

Blind as a bat. And as mad as a badger. Since then Mrs K often popped in, always with some story about her dead husband, Ivor, and her children, who were grown up now and never visited. She liked the company and Dirk was always careful not to let his scaly skin accidentally brush against her.

Also available:

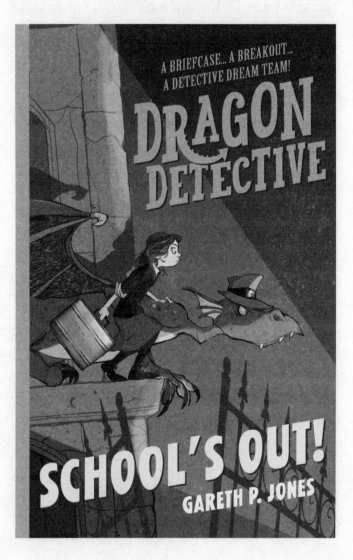

A BRIEFCASE... A BREAKOUT...
A DETECTIVE DREAM TEAM!

DRAGON
DETECTIVE

SCHOOL'S OUT!
GARETH P. JONES

About the Author

Gareth P. Jones is a Blue Peter Award-winning children's author of over 40 books for children of all ages, including *The Thornthwaite Inheritance*, *The Considine Curse* and *Death or Ice Cream*. His series fiction includes Ninja Meerkats, Adventures of the Steampunk Pirates, Pet Defenders and Dragon Detective.

Gareth regularly visits schools all over the world as well as performing at festivals. He plays ukulele, trumpet, guitar, accordion and piano to varying levels of incompetence. He lives in south-east London with his wife and two children.